STRANGE WIND

To Bernice,

Best Wishes

Jeffery Lamb

JEFFERY LAMB

Strange Wind
All Rights Reserved
Copyright 2004 by Jeffery Lamb

First printing……..…2004
Second printing….…2007

This book may not be reproduced, in whole or in part, in any manner without the written permission of the author.

This book is a work of fiction. Any resemblance to places, events, or actual persons, living or dead is entirely coincidental.

ISBN: 978-1-932672-38-1

A special thanks to:

Patricia Allegar, Editing

Bryan Riolo, Cover art

Novels by Jeffery Lamb

Youth

Save the Gator Queen

The Old Livingston House

<u>Coming Soon:</u>

Bugs Come Out at Night

Adult

Strange Wind

<u>Coming Soon:</u>

Margarita's in the Moonlight

For comments about this book or information on any Jeffery Lamb titles, contact the author at:

Jlambauthor@aol.com

DEDICATION

I'd like to dedicate this book to I.W. Lamb, my father. Dad passed away before I ever began writing, but I know that if he were here today, holding this book in his hands, he would look me right in the eyes and say, "You wrote a book? What a waste of time. Stop this nonsense and get a real job."

His love didn't always show through his rough exterior, but whether this book is a success or not, I've amounted to more than I ever should have and it's all because of him. Peace be with you Dad. Wish you were here.

CHAPTER 1

It was a warm afternoon, even with the rain coming down at Oak Park Cemetery just outside Orlando city limits. Raindrops fell lightly against the dark blue canvas covering the aluminum frame of the Morgan Funeral Home tent.

Frank Summers was still in shock as he stood under the small shelter. He refused to believe that his wife was gone, and he would never see her smile, or hear her laugh again. It was more than he could stand and he felt there was no way he could possibly go on with his life. Not without wonderful Karen by his side. For the last seventeen years, Karen had been Frank's whole world. She was the only thing he ever cared for, and the reason he was as successful as he was.

For over six years now he had been, and still was, the top car salesman at Tomasino Motors. None of the other seven salesmen ever came close to his performance. Everyday Frank put everything he had, not only into the job, but each individual sale. He treated every customer as if that person's satisfaction was his reason for living. All salesmen try, but unlike his colleagues he truly believed it. He always took the customer's side, to the point that Mike

Tomasino himself had to step in to keep the peace. Things became pretty heated between Frank and the sales manager on several occasions. Frank didn't care for his customers for who they were. He only cared about what they enabled him to do for his beloved Karen.

She was really a simple girl who had always been happy and cheerful in any situation. She was twenty-one when Frank met her at the state fair in Tampa. Karen was with two of her friends from the Community College and was standing in line for the roller coaster when he first saw her.

"Only two to a car you know?" Frank said, as he walked up behind her. He had gone there by himself, not to ride the rides, but hoping to land a job when it came time to tear them down. He was twenty-four and to carefree for his own good.

"I'll be riding solo, thank you." Karen said, not even turning around. Her friends in front of her laughed at her flirtatious smile.

"Well, I guess I'll be riding solo too, but it seems like a shame to make these nice people behind us have to wait for another turn when we could double up," Frank said, not being one to give up easily.

Karen still hadn't turned around while her friends were giggling uncontrollably. Now Karen was confused, some stranger had just made a comment that sounded exactly like something that she might say. Always wanting to consider the concerns of others was something Karen always tried to do.

"You know, you could just step out of line," she said in a joking manner. Karen had already deciding that she would let this person sit next to her on the ride, although she still had not seen him.

"I guess I could, but that wouldn't help at all. You would still be taking up a full seat by yourself," Frank said.

Picking up on the playfulness in her voice he decided to press forward. "You know we could both step out of line and let me buy you a Coke while your friends ride."

Her friends where struggling to not laugh out loud. For some unknown reason they seemed to find it extremely funny that their friend was getting hit on by a good looking stranger. Karen decided that this had gone far enough, she turned around.

She was beautiful. She had long dark hair and deep green eyes that looked as if they had never seen a moment of sadness. Frank stepped back. He knew she had a nice ass, but this was more than he could have every hoped for. Hell, he didn't even like roller coasters, especially the ones that went upside down like this one did. She just happened to be the last girl standing in line as he walked by. Frank would have done the same thing if it would have been either one of her friends, or just about any girl that happened to be the third girl in line for a two-person ride. He had the attitude that you never pass up an opportunity to try to get what you want, and he wanted a girlfriend. He wanted a job too, but mostly a girlfriend. The fact was he knew no decent girl would have anything to do with a guy that didn't have a job. He also knew that the more times you took a shot at your goal the sooner you achieved it. He never in his wildest dreams thought he would find someone like Karen. Frank thought she was the prettiest girl he had ever seen. The smell of popcorn and Italian sausage only added to the moment.

Karen was slightly knocked off guard herself when she turned around. Frank was handsome in a plain sort of way. He had black wavy hair that barely touched his collar, average build and brown eyes. His attitude seemed to shine brightly through his smile. That must be what her friends saw to make them act the way they did.

From that moment on hardly a day went by the two of

them didn't see each other or at least talk on the phone. When they did talk on the phone, it was usually about when they would see each other again.

    Now after seventeen years of complete happiness she was gone. There was not even a chance to say goodbye, talk or laugh one more time. If he could Frank would have given up his eyesight for one last embrace. The preacher finished, and closed his Bible, then with a bowed head turned and headed out into the rain. You could hear the sound of the folding metal chairs being relieved of their duty as people rose to find their way back to their cars.

    Soon, Frank was the only person left standing outside the tent, hoping maybe the rain would wash away some of the pain inside him. Raindrops mixed with tears to form a shallow puddle at his feet. He turned toward the lane inside the cemetery where he had parked his Town Car. He stared at it as the drops of rain danced along its top and hood, appearing to form a halo around the car. The Lincoln's size alone was impressive, not to mention its strong lines. Frank was finding it hard to walk toward the car. If Karen would have taken the Town Car instead of the two-seater convertible, she loved so much maybe she would still be alive. The thought flashed through his mind again, as he had pictured a hundred times over the last few days.

    She'd been driving down Orange Avenue to pick up her friend Sherri for their weekly assault on Orlando's finest yard sales. Frank had worked hard to get them to the point in their life where nothing within reason was out of reach for them financially. Of course Karen had her own agenda. It was a big part of what made him love her so much. As the little BMW convertible crossed Florida Street a pickup truck with faulty brakes, came speeding through a red light and now his whole life would never be the same.

    Frank struggled to get his mind back to reality and off the memory of that awful day. Once he regained control of his thoughts, he found himself sitting behind the wheel of the car with the ignition key in his hand. The door half open, and his left was foot still making contact with the wet pavement outside. Frank forced himself to put the key in the ignition and start the car. Tears formed in his eyes once again and he felt lost, not knowing what to do. Pulling out of the cemetery was going to be hard enough; leaving Karen behind is something he never thought he would have to face. He felt that if he stayed there long enough someone would come and wake him up from this bad dream. He knew that was not the case, since the accident three days ago he had not gone to work, not answered the phone, or eaten. He didn't even know which way to turn when he got to the end of the lane. He couldn't go home, that would be to hard. Getting something to eat might be a good start, he thought.

Other than Karen he pretty much liked to be alone. He didn't even know where most of the guys that he worked with for years lived, much less the names of their wives. They all knew Karen, because she had always been his favorite subject of conversation around the showroom.

Unlike the other wives, it was not unusual for her to stop by the car lot and pick up Frank for lunch or just sit and talk at his desk during times when business was slow.

One of her favorite pastimes would happen when she'd hear a new sales manager had been hired. An event that took place more often than Mike Tomasino felt was necessary. Karen would show up at the lot and pretend to be an irate customer of Frank's. The other salesmen knew it would be coming and made quite the effort to be on the showroom floor when it happened. Frank knew it would happen too, but never exactly when. Everyone would keep an eye out for the little blue two-seater to pull up in front of the showroom window. Then it was time to find your seat, the show was about to begin. Of course Frank played the part of the shocked salesmen perfectly not to disappoint the fun loving Karen.

It began as a fuming Karen headed straight to the manager's office. Everyone did their best to keep a straight face. Soon Karen, followed by the new sales manager, would come out of his office heading straight for Frank's desk. Every manager had the same look of bewilderment on his face. Then the moment the guys were all waiting for; what kind of unbelievable problem was Karen having with the make-believe car that Frank had supposedly sold her.

"Frank," every manager started the same way, and in the same state of shock.

"This nice lady here says the car you sold her last week is at the bottom of the St. Johns River, because you guaranteed that it could float and she'd never have to wait on a drawbridge again. Is that true?"

"Hey, I told her whatever it took to make the sale." Frank would brush off the complaint. "That's how we do it here."

"Bu… bu… but Frank!" The new guy would really be starting to sweat now.

"I'll tell you what," Karen would step in; "I'll just take my down payment out in trade with this salesman." Stepping behind Frank's desk she would give him a big hard kiss while the manager stood there watching with his mouth open. Karen was a lot of fun no doubt, and Frank and her where the perfect match.

Once again, Frank had to force his mind back to reality.

"Yes sir, can I help you?" The voice of a young woman was coming from a speaker pointing directly at his driver side window.

"Oh, um, yes a number three value meal with a Coke please," Frank answered.

Apparently he had managed to leave the cemetery and

find his way to a fast food joint. Not knowing how he did it, he felt proud of himself for making such a small step toward moving on with his life.

"How are you today sir?" A teenage girl said as he pulled up to the window. She had long blonde hair and braces on her teeth.

"I'm just fine." Frank lied.

He took the paper bag and Coke she was holding and pulled out of the drive thru.

A department store with a large parking lot sat next to Burger World. Frank pulled into one of the parking spots and shut off the car. The last time Frank had been on this side of Orlando was about twelve years ago. He and Karen had seen an ad in the newspaper for a used sixteen-foot fiberglass boat. The old boat ended up being a big part of their lives for almost three years. Finally, the engine blew up one summer on Lake Harris near the city of Leesburg. It was about two o'clock and the rain was still falling. Frank sat in the car and ate his lunch. Although he hadn't eaten much these last few days, he was unable to finish the burger and fries. His appetite just wouldn't allow it.

Frank got out of the car and started walking across the parking lot. He thought he would buy himself a new shirt and try to get used to the feeling of being around other people. It was something he never feared before, but now it seemed strange and awkward to him. He was glad to be in a place he had never been, so nothing inside would bring back memories of him and Karen being in a familiar place together.

As Frank walked toward the men's clothing section he could hear two small children trying to talk their mother into buying them something from the toy department. It made him think of why he and Karen never had children. They had talked about it several times over the years, but the timing just never felt right.

With his mind on Karen, Frank wasn't paying attention to where he was going until he found himself in the lingerie section. The sight and smell of the fabric made the memories flow. He would never want to forget any detail about Karen or their life together. He just needed some time to adjust to being without her. Now, he no longer had anyone to depend on, to care for and to bring gifts home to but himself. That's why he thought of buying a new shirt. It would be a gift to himself for making it through this hard time. A new shirt would be one thing in the house that had no feelings attached to it.

Frank found the men's section and located a rack of the type of shirts he liked. They were button down with a collar, but mostly over done with bright colors. After walking half-way around the rack; he picked up a blue one with a couple dozen other colors haphazardly spread across it. Frank looked inside the collar to see if it was a medium, it was, perfect just what he was hoping to find. On the rack next to the blue shirts was some of the same style only they were green. He thumbed though them until he located an M inside the collar. He held each one up against his chest and looked down at them. Not exactly sure why, but he had seen Karen do it every time they went shopping together.

Karen would pick out a blouse and hold it up in front of her.

"How does this look?" she would ask, like his opinion would be different if she had just held it up by the hanger.

"I don't know. It's hard to tell with those pants," Frank would answer, not being serious. "Why don't you slip them off and let me see how that would look?" Karen would roll her eyes at him and either put it back on the rack or head to the dressing room with it. One time she put the blouse back on the rack, pulled her pants down and stuck her tongue out at him. She was just being her playful self; luckily there was not a lot of people in the store.

Frank often referred to the incident as, 'his favorite day of shopping.'

Erasing the bittersweet memory Frank decided on both of the shirts he was holding. A quick glance at the price tag and he headed for the cash register.

After getting back in his car with the shopping bag, the lingering smell of French Fries made him feel like he had accomplished enough for one day. Frank wondered if it would be a good time to retrieve his things from the hotel he'd stayed at the last three nights. He had rented a room a couple of miles from their home, but tonight he would try to stay in the cold, lonely house.

CHAPTER 2

The house itself didn't pose a problem for Frank. It was like a thousand other three bedrooms, two bath homes throughout the Orlando area, but that was before Frank and Karen moved in. They bought the house not long after they were married. Every since then it had become Karen's labor of love. She spent most of her time making it more than just the place they lived. She worked to create an atmosphere that could only be fully appreciated by the two of them. A house with attitude is how they liked to describe it and its off-beat furnishings.

Frank opened the front door and stepped inside the house for the first time as an unmarried man. The first thing that caught his eye was the glass of watered down whiskey and Coke. He had just sat down to enjoy it, when he first received the news of the accident and rushed off to the hospital.

The drink was sitting on an end table that appeared to be an elephant's foot. It was a ceramic replica Karen had located at a second-hand store in Daytona. They only had the one, but Karen was the only person Frank had ever met that looked for one end table at a time. The table at the other end of the overstuffed leather couch was a yellow smiley face with a flat head. Each table was adorned with peach colored lamps. Frank was not sure what was supposed to match and what was not according to Karen. All he knew was whatever he suggested was going to be wrong.

    Whenever she brought home something new, or painted one wall a different color than the rest of the room, he would joke about setting up an appointment with a shrink, or maybe just commit her to the mental hospital. It seemed like something was different in the house every time he came home, but deep down he liked the changes, and Karen knew it.

    Frank quickly picked up the glass and carried it into the kitchen. He set it upside down in the sink, as if the faster the contents went down the drain the sooner the pain of that awful night would subside. He stood facing the sink with his hands resting on the counter top. Soon the gurgling sound from the drain stopped and Frank realized how quiet the house had become.

    He walked back into the living room and turned on the television. Some noise, some voices of other people may help to relieve the sickening feelings of loneliness. Frank flipped through the channels with the remote. It didn't matter what was on just so it wasn't depressing or involved happy loving couples. There lying on the coffee table, which resembled a sleeping mermaid with a glass top resting across her sculptured body, was the shopping bag. He looked at the bag knowing what it contained meant a trip to the bedroom. Even worse, opening the closet and touching or even seeing the clothes that used to cover the beautiful body of his late wife. Clothes that now hung with no use whatsoever, other than to remind him of how much he was going to miss her.

    Frank picked up the bag, and headed back to the kitchen instead. Frank thought a drink would help settle his nerves. He slowly brought the items together; the glass, ice, Coke, a bottle of Jack Daniel's from the cabinet. Pouring a shot of the whiskey into the glass Frank decided to skip the Coke. He took a deep breath, like he was about to attempt to lift a heavy object. Putting the glass to his lips, and with a quick tilt of his head, the glass was empty. He took the bag he had carried into the kitchen off the counter and headed for the bedroom.

Walking down the hallway seemed like a scene from a movie. This wasn't really happening, at least not to him. The door to the bedroom was open as always. Frank turned on the light even though it was not dark outside. The sun would be setting soon but the room was still bright.

The closet had a double sliding mirror for a door. The side closest to the door was full of all of Karen's things, and on the other side was more of Karen's things with a small space near the wall just for Frank. He carefully slid the door open to expose his ten percent of the space. Frank lifted two hangers from the bar and turned to the bed where the new shirts laid. He grabbed the dangling price tag on the green one and started to pull it off when thoughts of Karen overtook him once again. Only this time the tears did not follow, instead a smile spread across his lips, along with a half a laugh, as he could picture Karen scolding him in her teasing manner.

"Don't do that, you'll rip the shirt. Go and get the scissors and cut the tags off."

He rolled his eyes toward the heavens and walked into the bathroom to get the scissors. Returning to the bed, he clipped off the tags then hung the shirts in the closet. Making sure he put the scissors back where they belonged in the drawer next to the sink. That was the way Karen would have wanted it.

After returning to the kitchen he made himself a drink, with Coke this time. He walked into the living room to check the answering machine for the first time in three days. It was loaded as expected. Frank hit the button and sat back in his recliner next to a three foot tall African Witch Doctor. It was made of dark wood with jute hair that served no purpose other than a good scare in the middle of the night every now and then. Karen had spotted it in a gift shop last year during a day trip to St. Petersburg and decided she just had to have it. The calls were about what Frank expected. Some concerned neighbors, worried family members, and a few from friends. A couple of the guys from work had called to see if there was anything they could do, and kept him abreast of what was going on at the car lot. After the recorded messages stopped, Frank refilled his drink, making it a little stronger than he normally cared for then returned to the recliner. He lowered the volume on the television and resolved to sleep in the living room for the first few nights knowing the bedroom would be much too difficult.

CHAPTER 3

    Frank found himself waking up in the recliner the next morning. He had made it through his first night in the big, lonely house. Night time had been the hardest part, the time that he missed Karen the most. The evenings he had spent at the hotel seemed to have lasted forever. During the day he could always step outside and see someone jogging, or walking their dog. At night, by himself he felt more alone than he had his whole life. Frank slowly stood up, as the sun filtered through the blinds, and the anxiety of the first night in the now joyless home was behind him.
    The television was still on from the night before. He reached for the remote lying on the end table. Frank noticed his glass from last night was sitting on a coaster, "just like Karen had taught him," he thought. With a smile he turned off the television.
    What day was it? He wondered, Wednesday, no Thursday. It wasn't Friday was it? No, it had to be Thursday. The time, what time was it? Time hadn't meant much lately. Frank couldn't remember the last time he'd looked at a clock. "It must be seven, seven thirty," he thought, Frank gave a puzzled look at the clock hanging on the wall. It was a photograph of Elvis with clock hands

sticking out of his guitar revealing that it was a quarter past nine.

Frank dragged himself to the bathroom. He turned on the water in the shower and began to undress. For the first time realizing he had slept in the suit he'd worn to the funeral the day before. The same one he'd worn in the pouring rain. Realizing this, he was surprised that he had been able to sleep as well as he did. Frank slipped off the jacket and pulled down his slacks. They came off like cardboard, stiff and awkward, with a slight smell of mildew. Frank gathered the clothing up off the furry purple rug, shaped like a giant bare foot. He was about to toss them into the wicker hamper when he could once again hear the voice of his angel.

"Don't put wet clothes in the hamper!" Again it made him smile.

He had loved Karen unconditionally with every ounce of his being. The thought of them not being together, for even a second over the last seventeen years, never crossed his mind. Four days ago he saw no way of surviving without her. All he had hoped for was to be able to survive, not live a normal life, but just survive the devastating blow of her being taken so suddenly.

Now he stood there naked on a purple hang-ten rug. He had an eight-hundred dollar suit that smelled like cat food, wadded up in his hands. A small glimmer of hope was starting to pry its way into his mind, that he would somehow make it.

After a long hot shower, Frank put on a pair of shorts, tennis shoes and one of the new shirts. He made his way to the kitchen and poured himself a glass of orange juice; the day ahead didn't look too bad. If Frank could only think of something to do, some place to go to keep his mind occupied. To keep it from wandering back to how much he missed his wife. He walked into the living room, trying to come up with someplace he could go to get out of the empty house. While coming up with a plan to fill the empty day the phone rang. After the second ring Frank decided to answer it.

"Hello?" Frank managed weakly.

"Hello, Frank? It's me Mike, how are you doing?" The surprised voice of Mike Tomasino came though the receiver.

"I'm doing okay I guess," Frank answered.

"I didn't know if you would be home or not. I left a couple of messages on your answering machine just to see how you were," Mike said.

He was trying to sound like his own interest was the reason for the call. They had been friends for a long time.

"I've been staying at the Palm Tree Hotel for the last few days. I haven't returned any calls yet," Frank said hoping Mike wouldn't think he had been avoiding him.

"Understood, understood, I just wanted to see if there was anything we could do for you, or if you needed someone to talk to. You know you can take all the time you need. No need to rush back, your job will always be here waiting for you." Mike said.

"Thanks Mike, but how about if I come in for a few hours today?" Frank said, not sure why.

Mike pulled the phone away from his ear. He looked at the receiver like it was trying to pull a practical joke on him. He quickly realized how foolish he must look he put it back to his head.

"Um, um, sure Frank, whatever you want to do, I mean it, it's up to you."

"I don't know what else to do with myself Mike; I think I'll come to work. I probably won't be worth a damn, but I'd like to come in, I think."

"Okay Frank, that's fine with me, I guess I'll see you in a little while." Mike said, realizing how Frank must be feeling.

Frank looked in the mirror. It was not what he would normally wear to work, but today this was the best he was going to pull together. Frank got into his Town Car and drove the route he had driven so many times before. This time the thrill of possibly making big commissions didn't enter his head. It wasn't long before he was pulling into the parking lot of Tomasino's motors. Tom and Phil, two salesmen and Rita, a lady that worked in the office, were standing outside having a cigarette. They watched Frank's silver Town Car pull in and straddle the yellow line dividing the parking spaces. Frank didn't realize he was taking up two spaces, and no one felt it necessary to point it out to him. The smoking trio proceeded down the concrete ramp to the parking area, not knowing what was happening. No one expected him back to work so soon. Frank noticed the small group of colleagues making their way toward him as he opened the door of the car. He really didn't know Rita very well. She had only been at Tomasino's for a couple of months. He liked Phil, but Tom had always been a little rude to him. It was not that he didn't like Frank; he was a little rude with everyone. He had just stepped out of the car when they reached him and the question of who would break the silence was soon answered.

"Hey, Frank. It's good to see you. Are you making it okay?" Tom said with true sincerity. Rita gently put her arm around Frank's neck.

"I'm so sorry to hear about your wife," she said, and kissed him gently on the cheek. Rita stepped back to where Tom and Phil were standing.

"It's good to see you Frank," Phil said, extending his hand.

"I didn't know what to do with myself, so I came here. Mike called me this morning. He knows I'm coming in."

Frank was still holding onto Phil's hand. Phil was looking for something to say.

"Well things have been kind of slow today so far."
They started walking toward the ramp.

"Thursdays usually are," Frank answered.

It was Wednesday but no one said anything. He made his way to his desk shaking hands and telling people thank you.

Once the commotion settled down Frank just sat at his desk. His shot at a customer only came up once that day, but he decided to let one of the other salesmen have it. He wasn't in the mood to sell just yet, but appreciated being put back on the rotation so quickly.

He took a few phone calls from former customers setting up times for them to bring their cars in for service. He bought a box of Girl Scout cookies from a little girl who came into the showroom. He fielded a couple of sales calls but nothing important. Mike came by his desk and sat with him for about twenty minutes. They talked about some design changes he heard of on the new cars coming out of Detroit, and how the fishing was last weekend over at Lake Monroe. Frank made it until closing time.

On the way home he stopped by a small bar he had been driving by for years. He had a drink just to prolong the time until he would be alone. When he got home he turned on the television and went to sleep in the recliner.

CHAPTER 4

Frank woke in the middle of the night. With his eyes barely opened he quickly surveyed the dimly lit room. "Something must have caused him to wake up," he thought. The wind blew through the trees in the front yard causing the light from the streetlamp to appear to flicker. A strange banging noise came from outside. If someone was trying to break in, Frank wondered if he would even try to defend his property. With Karen gone what else would even matter? Frank pulled the blanket up over his shoulder and attempted to roll over. That's when he saw that someone was inside the house, causing him to care again. Frank couldn't tell which way the burglar was facing, but could see he was crouched down looking for something. He slowly moved down in the chair until he could reach the poker from the hearth of the fireplace. Frank crept up behind the thief. He brought the metal rod down with all his strength, making contact with the man's head. When he turned on the light, Frank realized he had split the African Witch Doctor in two. He looked out the window through the blinds and watched the neighbor's basset hound running from his porch. A sad smile crossed his face as he looked down at the two halves of the wooden statue. Sad that he had destroyed something of Karen's but at the same time he knew she would laugh out loud if she had been there to see him. He stepped over the statue and replaced the poker in its stand. "One less thing to remind him of her," he thought. It wasn't easy around the house after being together so long. Everything they owned they had acquired since they had been together. Everything in the house served as a reminder of how much he missed her.

    When he looked at the zebra striped couch he could not see it for what it was, just an old couch. No, he pictured the way he and Karen struggled to get it in through the front door when they moved in. He pushed, she pulled. She pushed, he pulled. He pulled while she sat on it. They took off all the cushions and turned it up on its end. Laughing and giving each other kisses the whole time. He also relived the time they snuggled up on it to watch a horror movie. She almost scared them both to death with a flashlight, a bed sheet, and a squeeze bottle of ketchup. She always did have a twisted sense of humor. Frank fell back into his recliner, and with some effort, was able to get back to sleep.

    Frank's neck was a little stiff when he woke the next morning. It was not the most comfortable way to spend the night, but he still could not bring himself to sleep in the queen size bed down the hall. After a quick shower and a cup of coffee he was feeling much better. Frank dressed for work hoping today would be the day he pulled it together, and moved on with his life.

    Frank sat at his desk and stared out the window at the passing cars. A blue convertible came up the road. Frank imagined it was Karen and she was coming to tell him everything was going to be fine. He looked down at his desk as the sporty little car passed by.

    It wasn't long before an older gentleman came shuffling

into the showroom and asked for Frank by name. His name was Mr. Douglas and he had a friend at the Moose Club who had bought a pickup truck from Frank a few months ago. The friend had recommended Frank highly. Most of the sales Frank made were from referrals by happy customers he had sold cars to in the past. Mr. Douglas was tired of the car he had. It was a seven-year-old midsize and he thought he would be happier with a newer full size car. Frank walked with Mr. Douglas around the lot showing him several different models of luxury cars. They looked inside of a two-year-old Cadillac.

"Cadillac has never been my style," Mr. Douglas said with a laugh.

"Style's a funny thing Mr. Douglas," Frank began. "I don't have much of it myself." He couldn't help but smile as he thought of Karen and the touch of class that she had added to his life.

"Oh, I didn't say I don't have any style; it's not Cadillac style. No, my style is more, easy going," Mr. Douglas looked across the roof of the Cadillac at Frank. Frank rubbed his chin.

"You know what Mr. Douglas; it sounds to me like you have Mercury style. Come with me, I'd like to show you something."

Frank led the way through the garage area to the back lot. A Grand Marquis had been traded in a few days ago and was waiting to be detailed.

Even though the energy level wasn't what it used to be, the Grand Marquis was driving off the lot with another happy customer.

David Jones, a middle aged man who owned a small Italian restaurant, pulled into Tomasino's in his red Camaro. Frank had sold him the car just before Karen's accident. It was the third vehicle David had purchased from Frank. It seemed that every time he got a new girlfriend; he felt he should have a new car. However, the latest restaurant queen was still hanging in there because he was only there for new brake shoes. You would have thought he owned a chain of restaurants by the way he walked in the showroom jingling his keys. His shirt was one size too small and the top three buttons were unfastened, exposing his collection of gold chains.

"Hey Frank, how are you? I heard about your wife, I'm sorry," David said. He sat down in front of Frank's desk.

"I'm doing fine I guess, a little lost around the house, but other than that I'm fine," Frank said leaning back in his chair. "What brings you by today?"

"I have an appointment with the service department at eleven o'clock for a brake job," David answered.

"How is Darla doing?" Frank asked hoping that was the name of the last girlfriend he had been introduced to.

"She's doing great. She's so hot I can't even let her go in the walk-in cooler at the restaurant without her melting the cheese, if you know what I mean." David was leaning his forearms on Frank's desk and giving him a wink. Even in Frank's current mood, David made him smile.

"I've got one of my waiters picking me up so I can get back in time for the lunch time rush. Could you pull my car around when they're ready for her?"

"Sure Dave, no problem," Frank said, taking the keys from him.

"Thanks Frank. Stop by the restaurant later and I'll buy you lunch," David said. A young man in a beat up Honda pulled up beside the Camaro.

David walked outside and jumped into the passenger side. The Honda shook like a dog coming in out of the rain and away they went. Frank laughed to himself and jingled the keys in his hand.

He was up next so the next person at the lot was his customer. Frank stepped out the door when he noticed a young couple in their early twenties bent over looking in the windows of an older pickup on the back row. He made his way down the ramp toward them. Frank introduced himself.

"Good morning, my name is Frank. Is there something I can help you with?"

"We're just looking today," the young man said; standing up straight, but still looking at the truck.

Frank noticed a wedding band on the girl's left hand and saw the disinterested look on her face. He knew that this wasn't going to go very far. Frank thought back to when he had first married Karen, and how hard money was to come by. He would probable have bounced around from one low paying job to another, if it had not been for Karen. Her love for him had given him the desire to make something of his life. Frank wanted to give her everything she wanted, and that's exactly what he did.

"Well here's my card. If you have any questions that I can help you with just let me know. If not have a good day and come back and see me when you're ready to drive one of these home."

The young man took the card from Frank and looked at it. With nine years of experience Frank knew not to offend or be forceful with anyone. For all he knew the kid could have ten thousand dollars in his pocket even though it didn't look like he had ten. Frank knew that you made more money that way. He stepped back inside the showroom and watched to see what the young couple's next move might be. After looking at a couple more trucks, he watched them get into their car and drive away.

Looking down, Frank realized that he was still holding David's Camaro keys. He went over to his desk and called the service manager.

"Service department, this is Dale." A man's voice came through the receiver.

"Hey Dale it's Frank. I've got David Jones's Camaro up here. Can I bring it back for the brake job?" Frank asked.

"Yeah Frank, sure, bring it on back. One of the guys just finished changing a timing belt and can start on it right after lunch."

"Okay great, I'll pull it around." Frank hung up the phone and walked out of the showroom. When he opened the car's door the smell of a pine scented air freshener almost made Franks eyes water. The Fantasy Fest beads hanging from the rearview mirror gently swayed as Frank took a seat. Frank smiled to himself, as he started up the car.

After a few seconds music from the stereo filled the interior of the clean little car. Frank carefully backed it out of the parking space then shifted the car into drive heading toward the garage. He found himself entranced by what was coming out of the speakers. He'd always enjoyed all types of music, country, to jazz; to rock and roll, but this was something different. He couldn't even make out what kind of instruments the band was playing. A man's voice accompanied the odd sounding band with calm, laid back, vocals that seemed happy and relaxed.

"Trade winds blowing over the bow of my boat; have another drink and along we will float. From the mainland to the islands and back again, me, a margarita and my new girl friend."

The song's simple rhythm flowed effortlessly around Frank, as he pulled the car into the garage bay. He cut off the engine, and handed the keys to Eddie, the mechanic who had just guided him in. Eddie walked around the car adjusting the arms of the hydraulic lift so he could begin his work. Frank sat in the car for a moment before heading back to the showroom.

Back at his desk Frank picked up the sports page of the Orlando Sentinel to see if the Buccaneers had won or lost last Sunday. He might have watched the game on television, but he couldn't remember. After learning they had won and glancing through the rest of the paper, he decided to go to lunch.

In the corner of the shopping center, across the street from Tomasino's Motors, was a sub shop. Frank had not been to it before despite working so close to it for the last nine years. It would be a good time to try it since it had no ties to Karen. Frank walked to the curb and waited for traffic to clear before crossing the street. The shop was small with only three or four tables, but it was clean and brightly lit. Two ladies were seated at one of the tables, and a young man with a paper hat on his head stood behind the counter. Frank stood back from the counter a few feet to view the menu.

"Hey, Johnny Branson!" The counter man said as he looked at Frank.

"I'm sorry, excuse me," Frank said, thinking the man had mistaken him for someone else.

"Trade winds blowing over the bow of my boat," that's a Johnny Branson tune you're humming, I'm a big fan," the young man said. Was he humming? Frank didn't realize he had been humming.

"Oh, um is that who sings that song?" Frank mumbled, caught off guard.

"He don't just sing it man, he lives it. I have all of his CD's. When I retire, I'll be right out there with him in the Gulf of Mexico. On my own boat, with a bottle of rum and a blonde who is dumb. Now, what can I get for you sir?" The man talked with excitement in his voice as Frank refocused on the menu.

"I guess I'll have a ham and cheese on whole wheat

with a large Coke." Frank was finding it hard to believe that he was humming but he must've been. The young man went to work on the sandwich singing the song Frank had been humming. He was not nearly as good as the man Frank had heard in the Camaro.

"Let's see. That will be $4.85," he said when he had finished wrapping up the sub. Frank laid a ten-dollar bill on the counter and stuck a straw through the slit in the lid of the cup. The young man made change and put the ten in the cash register. Frank let the five-dollar bill lay on the counter.

"Put that toward your boat," Frank said with a smile, and turned for the door.

"My Lucky Star thanks you sir," the young man said. He held the five-dollar bill up in front of him with both hands. Frank looked back puzzled

"That's what I'm naming my boat when I get her," he said, "The Lucky Star," smiling he kissed the five dollar bill and tucked it into his shirt pocket.

Frank took his lunch and went back across the street to Tomasino's. He continued to hum the goofy little song. After finishing his sandwich Frank picked up the Coke and walked out into the garage. The large building was quiet with everyone gone for lunch. David's Camaro was raised slightly off the floor sitting on the lift. Frank opened the driver's door. He reached inside and pushed the eject button on the stereo. Out popped the white edge of the cassette tape. He pulled it out and placed his drink on the roof of the car. 'Johnny Branson's Greatest Hits' was stamped in bold type across the tape. Frank turned the tape over and began looking at some of the names of the songs. Sailing into the Sunset, Your Island or Mine, A Bottle of Rum and a Blonde who is Dumb. This was apparently, where the sandwich maker had gotten his comment. When Frank was about to put the cassette back into the stereo.

He noticed a tape case wedged in between the seat and the console. He pulled it out into the open. It was the one that belonged to the tape he held in his other hand. On the cover of the case was a picture of a man about Frank's age, 42. The smiling man was sitting under a palm tree on the beach with a guitar in his hands. Two young ladies in string bikinis were playing with a beach ball in the background. Frank put the tape back into the stereo, and the little case where he had found it. He closed the door and went back to his desk.

No one bought a vehicle from Frank that day, and for the first time in his career he didn't care. He had caught himself humming several times while talking with three different car shoppers but no sales. The island song stuck in his head all day.

When Frank left Tomasino's that evening he drove to the super store on 5th Street, and walked back to their music section.

"Excuse me, but can you tell me if you have any Johnny Branson CD's?" He asked a tall brunet woman dusting off a rack of video games with a feather duster.

"Yes, I believe we do," she said as she slid past Frank, and walked up the next aisle.

"Here they are." She pointed with the duster then teasingly gave them a quick cleaning. She smiled at Frank and went back to her work.

"Thank you," he said as she walked away. The selection was small, about four or five different titles. Frank picked up the greatest hits CD without even examining it. He thought he would buy a couple different ones to give himself a full taste of the singer's talent. On the cover of his second selection it showed Johnny standing on the deck of a boat with a fishing pole in one hand, and holding up a tall tropical looking drink with the other. A pink bikini top was hanging from the fishing pole and an attractive young lady in pink bikini bottoms with her arms covering her breast was standing beside him. The picture showed both of them with big smiles on their faces. The title of the CD, *Sails, Whales, and Cocktails* was printed above their heads on a rainbow.

"Did you find what you were looking for?" the brunette asked as Frank laid the CDs on the counter.

"Yes I think so," he answered. She scanned the two CDs and put them in a plastic bag. Frank handed her his credit card and waited for his receipt.

Once back in the car Frank took the cellophane off the greatest hits CD, and inserted it into the stereo. When the music began Frank immediately smiled when the song that had been on his mind most of the day came spilling out of the Lincoln's speakers. The seventh song had just finished when Frank pulled into the driveway.

After seeing there were no messages on the answering machine, he placed the CD in the stereo. Then he mixed a drink, which he decided from now, would be referred to as a cocktail, like Johnny did on the other CD. Next, he dragged the mattress out of the bedroom and laid it on the living room floor. He picked up the two pieces of the wooden witch doctor and put them in the closet for its own protection. Frank listened to the two CDs a couple of times each and had one more cocktail. He drifted off to sleep while the songs of a carefree lifestyle played into the night.

CHAPTER 5

Frank realized how big the mattress was as he awoke the next morning. Without Karen snuggled up against him he felt like he was stranded on a deserted island. As he showered and dressed he thought of taking the day off, maybe go to the beach or head up to St. Augustine for some sightseeing. Logic took over and he decided on going to work since the weekend was coming up. He would need something to fill the empty hours looming before him. It wasn't long ago he couldn't wait for the weekends to come so Karen and he could spend the time together, but now he dreaded the lonely hours.

On his way to Tomasino's, Frank stopped to fill up with gas. Inside he noticed a rack of magazines advertising different things for sale. Frank spotted one named *Nothing But Boat,* and, he thought it would give him something to occupy his time when things were slow.

"I'll take this too," Frank laid the magazine on the counter.

"Certainly sir," the man at the register said. Frank thought back to the old bow rider he and Karen had spent so much time on years ago and smiled. They had cruised just about every lake and canal in central Florida; until the old outboard blew up on Lake Harris near Leesburg. A fisherman, who had to much to drink, and not enough fish to catch that afternoon, towed them back to the boat ramp.

Frank was the second salesman to arrive at Tomasino's that morning. Phil was on the lot with a middle-aged couple who was looking to buy a minivan. When Frank reached his desk a slender lady with short white hair, dressed in a light blue business suit came through the door.

"Could I use your phone please?" She asked.

"Sure, help yourself," Frank gestured to the one on his desk.

She dialed the phone quickly and then looked across the showroom while waiting for someone to answer. "Lisa, this is Barbara. Cancel my first two clients this morning. My piece of junk car broke down again and I'm not going to mess with it anymore. I'll be there as soon as I can. Okay bye." She hung up the phone and turned to Frank.

"I need a new car."

"What did you have in mind?" Frank asked.

"I don't know," she said. "I guess whatever you feel like selling me." Obviously she was very disgusted with her old car.

"Well, let me show you around a little and see if anything grabs your attention," Frank said somewhat surprised. No one had ever said, "Sell me whatever you want to," before. After a quick trip around the lot the woman pointed at a blue Mustang in the front row.

"What about that one over there?" she asked.

"The Mustang? That car is in great condition and it has very few miles on it. Would you like me to get the keys?" Frank asked.

"Oh it's no use; I don't know anything about cars." She hung her head slightly.

"Well at least that one matches your outfit," Frank said with a warm smile. She looked at Frank and smiled back.

"I guess that's as good as reason as any." She wasn't in the mood to negotiate. Frank offered to have her old car towed to the lot as part of the down payment.

She was in and out in about thirty minutes. He sat at his desk and looked at the magazine. After repeating the damsel in need of a car story a half dozen times to whoever asked. The morning was gone before he knew it.

Frank was thinking about whether or not to take David up on his free lunch offer when he overheard a conversation between Ricky and Tommy the sales manager. Ricky was one of the newer salesmen and had been showing the two-year-old Cadillac to a retired couple. They had driven up in an older model Toyota that looked brand new. The couple had made an offer for the Cadillac, but it looked like the deal was falling apart. Frank watched the older couple, still outside, walking slowly toward their Toyota. It seemed the deal wasn't going the way they had hoped.

"They want to trade the Toyota and a thirteen year old Bay Runner that's docked over in Crystal River." Ricky was saying.

"Are they out of their minds? We can't take a trade in on something we can't even get to the car lot. Tell them to go and sell the boat and then come back and see us."

"Bay Runner, Bay Runner," Frank thought as he thumbed though the pages of the magazine. Ricky was about to walk out the door to break the bad news to the folks.

"How big of a boat do they have?" Frank asked.

"I think they said it was a thirty-two foot cabin cruiser, whatever that is." Ricky said as the showroom door was closing behind him. Frank watched from his desk as Ricky and the senior citizens talked over the roof of their import. He couldn't hear the conversation. Frank watched as the man opened the car door, he had one leg in while still talking to Ricky. *"Trade winds over the bow of my boat."* The tune floated through Frank's head again. Maybe he should find out what was being said on the other side of the glass. He stepped out the door and moved slowly down the ramp.

"We used to take that thing everywhere didn't we Martha?" the man was saying. "Heck we lived on it for over three months when we traveled to the Virgin Islands back in ninety-four. We're starting to get a little too old to be out on the ocean for extended periods of time. That's what a boat that size is really designed for. I thought if we had a big comfortable car we might drive out to Las Vegas for a while, then just see where we end up."

"Well, I wish we could help you out but the boss isn't interested in a boat. Good luck though." Ricky was trying to get rid of them without being overly rude.

"How about a Town Car?" Frank blurted out. Everyone stopped to digest what was just said, even Frank.

"Well, that would be close to what we are looking for. What do you think Martha?" the man said shifting his eyes between Ricky, Frank, and Martha.

"It's that silver one over there," Frank said pointing to his own car.

The man and his wife looked toward the car.

"Why is it parked over there by itself?" Asked the potential customer, thinking maybe there was a problem with it.

"It's my own personal car," Frank said. Then he looked at Ricky and gave him a wink. "Ricky here mentioned you want to trade in a boat. I've been thinking about getting one myself. It sounds like from your description it's just what I'm looking for." Frank took the keys out of his pocket and walked over to the gentleman. "Here take it out for a drive and see what you think?" He placed them in the man's hand.

"Well, Martha what do you think? Should we take it for a spin?" The man said with a chuckle. Martha didn't say a word. She simply got out of the Toyota and made her way toward the Lincoln.

Frank watched as they walked toward his car and wondered how long they had been together. He had always counted on Karen growing old with him, now he felt like he would be alone forever. Frank knew the idea of a boat was crazy, he wished he could go inside and call his wife to get her opinion. It hurt to know that it was impossible. As fun loving as she was she had always been the voice of reason that kept him from doing dumb things like this.

When Frank came out of his trance the Town Car drove past him and Ricky and made a right turn into traffic.

"If I make this trade I'll give you a hundred dollars since they were your customers, okay?" Frank said.

"Um yeah, sure Frank that sounds fair," Ricky answered, since he had no other choice. Shortly after leaving the Lincoln came pulling back in and parked. Frank walked over as they were getting out.

"She seems like a fine car," said the driver. "I don't know if the boy told you or not that our boat is at a marina in Crystal River. We don't have anyway to bring it here."

"What kind of trade were you looking to make?" Frank asked, with the knowledge he had recently gained from the magazine at his desk. He knew that a boat that size and the car were close to the same value.

"Well, we have some money in the bank but I'd like to keep as much of it as we can. We also have that old

Toyota, it may not be worth much, but Martha don't drive you see."

"Tell me a little bit about your boat?" Frank asked.

"Well, it's a thirteen year old Bay Runner with a fly bridge, and it's fully self-contained. It's got everything; refrigerator, stove, shower, and its all in good shape. I bought it new and we haven't used it as much as we would have liked to. It doesn't have a lot of running time on the engines." The man was talking in a reminiscence manner. Frank looked at how well-kept the little Toyota was and figured the boat was probably in good shape.

"How about the boat, the Toyota, and two hundred dollars for the Town Car?" Frank said. The older man wasn't sure he heard correctly.

"What?" he exclaimed! "You haven't even seen the boat yet. Don't you want to at least drive over there and take a look at it?"

"I think I can trust you. You seem like an honest fellow to me," Frank said. The man and his wife looked at each other and laughed, they couldn't believe what was happening. It sounded good to them but things were moving awful fast. Frank noticed the puzzled look on their faces; he had seen it plenty of times before.

"You two want to talk it over? I'll be back in a few minutes." Frank walked back into the showroom to Mike Tomasino's office.

"Mike, I'm going to trade my car for the boat that Ricky was telling you about. If I do, is it alright if Rita does the title work for me?" Frank asked.

"Sure Frank, whatever you want, but why are you trading an almost new car for an old boat?" Mike said. That was a reasonable question. Frank only wished he could come up with a reasonable answer. The song floated though his head. It came in one ear and drifted out the other.

"Let's just say I want to feel the wind as it blows across the bow of my boat," Frank answered and left the office to go and close the deal.

"Feel the wind blow across the bow," Mike repeated Frank's words to himself. "What kind of answer is that? He shook his head and went back to his paperwork. Frank walked back out to the older couple. They had the hood up, but didn't know exactly what they were looking at.

"Well, what have you two decided?" Frank asked.

"We have decided we're leaving for Vegas Monday morning," the man said with a big smile.

After the changing of the titles, Frank walked out and looked at the tan Toyota that he now owned. It was nearing one o'clock so Frank decided to go for lunch. He got into the little car that seemed like a child's toy after driving the Lincoln for so long. The little engine sounded like a sewing machine as Frank headed up the road. It was no sports car, but it had more power and handled better than he expected. He circled the block then found his way to a parking spot in front of the sub shop across the street. The young man who had waited on him yesterday was ringing up an order for a lady with a little girl.

"Yes sir, how can I help you?" he said to Frank after the woman and child had gone.

"I'll have a Cuban sub and a large Coke." Frank noticed the man's badge read 'Hi my name is Bill.' "That Johnny Branson guy, how many albums has he put out?"

"Eight, counting his latest," Bill was wrapping up the Cuban. "Why do you ask?"

"Oh I bought a couple of them last night and I was just wondering how many there were." Frank took out his wallet to pay for his lunch.

"Hey all right, good for you man," Bill said. "I have all eight."

"They sure have a different sound to them." Frank

picked up his lunch and was just about to push open the door to the store.

"Not only that, they'll change your life," Bill said.

Frank looked out into the parking lot at the old Toyota.

"They already have." Frank smiled.

CHAPTER 6

Frank found Ricky when he returned from lunch and gave him the hundred dollars he had promised him.

"Thanks Frank. By the way what are you going to do with an old boat?" Ricky asked.

"I don't know, I really don't know," Frank answered. He wondered why he had done it and now that it was done, what to do next.

"Well, good luck with it whatever you do." Ricky put the money in his pocket and walked away. The rest of the day was pretty uneventful. Frank went home feeling pretty good even though he hadn't made a sale. He pulled his new car into the driveway. It looked small sitting in the spot where he was used to seeing the big Lincoln parked. The first thing he did when he got in the house was push the power button on the stereo and fix himself a cocktail.

Frank didn't sleep as late as he normally liked to on a

Saturday morning. He was eager to get to Crystal River and see what the hell he had done. He dressed in his regular weekend attire of walking shorts; tennis shoes, and a button-down shirt that if you spilled a plate of spaghetti on it, there was a good chance that no one would notice. After a glass of orange juice and a slice of toast, Frank grabbed his toolbox out of the garage and put it in the hatchback. He positioned himself as comfortably as possible in the tiny car seat and was off on a two hour drive to Crystal River.

The marina was located about a mile from where the mouth of the river opened up into the Gulf of Mexico. Frank pulled into the gravel parking lot of the marina; boats on trailers took up most of the lot. A blue and white metal building was sitting on the banks of the river. It consisted of a small area that displayed life jackets, marine batteries, air horns and other miscellaneous boat related items. Around back was a workshop area with two bays, a boat in each one. It reminded Frank of a scaled down model of Tomasino's. The showroom was in the front and a garage in the back, but for boats instead of cars. He walked around to the side of the building where he found a dock stretching out into the water with smaller docks sprouting off it on both sides. Frank looked at the bottom of the directions. D-8 was the slip-number of the boat's location. In Yellow weather-beaten paint, Frank noticed a large A painted on the walkway at the first intersection. It seemed obvious enough, when he came to D he turned right, 1, 3, 5, wrong way, he turned around. His heart was pounding as he stared at the 8 between his feet. What had he done, he looked up, his jaw dropped, something wasn't right. There must be some kind of mistake. He looked at the piece of paper D-8; he double checked the dock; D-8. "This couldn't be right," he thought. Maybe there is another dock on the other side of the garage. Frank walked toward the blue and white building. A man wiping his hands on a rag came out of the garage. He was wearing a mechanic's uniform and an old dirty baseball cap.

"Something I can help you with?" the man said, followed by the spitting of brown tobacco juice that made a splat sound as it hit the ground.

"Yes. I'm looking for a boat that's supposed to be docked at D-8 and…" Frank was interrupted at that point.

"You're looking for the Harris' yacht I bet?" No spit followed this time.

"Yes that's it. I'm looking for the Harris's yacht." Frank was not sure if there was a difference between a yacht and a boat. He liked the thought of owning a yacht. The same way he liked to drink a cocktail instead of a drink.

"Mr. Harris called yesterday and said they had made a deal with a Mr. Smithers."

"It's Mr. Summers," Frank corrected the tobacco-spitting mechanic, "Frank Summers."

"You didn't screw them did you?" More spit.

"Excuse me?" Frank wasn't sure he had heard the question correctly.

"I sure would hate to think someone took advantage of a couple of senior citizens. I thought a lot of the Harris's." This time no spit.

"I liked them myself." Frank answered. He wondered why this was becoming such a difficult conversation. "I honestly believe we made a deal that was good for everyone involved."

"Well I've been around boats all my life and I have never heard of anyone buying one without at least looking at it first," Splat! Wally said.

"Well I never heard of it either," Frank answered. "They seemed like such honest people I thought a drive from Orlando over here would be a waste of time." The mechanic changed his attitude somewhat. If Frank had trusted the Harris's enough to not even look the boat over, the only one who could get screwed would be Frank.

"I'm Wally Jensen," the mechanic said, extending his freshly wiped hand. "It's the *Don't Worry* you're looking for, it's right where it suppose to be. It's the white Bay Runner with orange trim docked at D-8."

Frank thought that the boat he had seen at D-8 was white with a small orange pinstripe down the hull.

"Oh, okay thanks, I just wanted to make sure I had the right one," Frank answered. When he reached the proper slip, he stared at the vessel. Near the stern, while walking along the wooden walkway he saw in orange script across the back, *Don't Worry*. That's the boat all right. He stepped aboard the boat as it rocked ever so slightly under his weight. He fished around in his pocket until he pulled out the key Mr. Harris had given him. It was attached to a green football shaped piece of foam rubber by a tiny chain. The final test occurred as Frank climbed the aluminum ladder to the bridge and slipped the key into the ignition, and gave it a turn. A masculine cough came from the engines and a continuous purr could be heard at the rear of the *Don't Worry*.

Frank made his way down the hatch and into the cabin. It was larger than he had expected it to be. A small stove was to his left with a microwave oven over head. A small refrigerator and a sink were next to it. In front of him was a U-shaped sofa with a table in the middle. To the right was a door that opened into a shower, toilet and tiny sink. Underneath the steps was a nice-sized sleeping area. The yacht he had never seen before, and now owned, was beautiful. He could not believe it was a thirteen-year-old boat. He felt the boat rock slightly and poked his head out of the cabin.

Wally had one foot on the gunwale with the other still

on the dock. "She's a little honey ain't she? The few times Buddy and Martha took her out for a cruise; they would have me go over everything when they got back. I know her pretty well, and there ain't anything wrong with her. You want me to untie her so you can run her out a bit? See how she does."

Frank was now standing on the deck. He grabbed the ladder leading up to the bridge.

"Yeah, I think I'll run up the coast a little ways," Frank said, locating the gas gauge first thing. He would hate to get stranded the first time out in his new boat. The gauge showed half a tank.

Wally tossed the last rope onto the deck. "Keep her off the sand bars," he called out, when the ropes were clear.

Frank slipped the throttle lever into reverse until the boat moved past the farthest point of the dock. Once it was clear, he headed in the direction of the ocean, pushing the lever forward giving her a little more gas. Moving along at a speed just above an idle, the boat seemed anxious to get to the ocean. Frank captained the yacht out of the river and steered the boat in a northern direction. He pushed the throttle down further and further until they were cruising along at a pretty good clip. The little yacht didn't skip a beat as man and machine got to know each other a couple of miles off shore. Soon Frank and his new friend the *Don't Worry* were farther north of the river than he had planned on. The wind blew through his hair, and the salty smell of the ocean filled his lungs. Maybe he could enjoy life on his own. After a few more sun-drenched miles he turned the craft around and headed back to the marina.

Frank pulled the boat alongside the marina gas pump and topped off the tank. Then he put his new boat back into slip D-8.

"How was the ride?" Wally asked, as Frank walked inside the marina to pay for the gas.

"Everything went fine," Frank answered.
"The rent on the slip is paid until the end of the month. Its one hundred and sixty-five dollars if you want to keep it here." Wally let Frank know.

Frank picked up a business card from the counter and stuck it in his wallet before returning it to his pocket.

"I don't know what I'm going to do yet. Mr. Harris had mentioned that he and his wife lived on it for a while." Frank said.

"I'll tell you what; if I owned a boat like that and could afford to get out of this rat race, my ass would be in the Keys by nightfall. I'd sell my trailer house and tell my boss to go to hell because I'm moving to paradise." Wally's voice got louder and faster as he spoke, like the thought might have crossed his mind before.

"The Keys, I've never been to the Keys," Frank said aloud, but in a way that sounded like he was thinking about it in his head.

"Me either," Wally said still excited. "I hear in Key West, after dark, the women run around naked."

Frank didn't think that was true, but he had heard of some pretty wild nights down there during Fantasy Fest.

"Well I have until the end of the month to decide I guess," Frank said. He took one last look at his yacht, then got back in his little car, and headed back to Orlando.

During the drive back, Frank thought about whether or not he had the finances to retire at forty-two.

Being the top salesman at Tomasino's Motors had made life damned comfortable. They had been working toward an early retirement for several years now. Frank had been shooting for fifty-five. He had been putting the maximum into his IRA, and having some pretty good luck with some blue chip stocks that he had been investing in steadily. Now he only had himself to support. The numbers in his head and Johnny Branson songs were blending together into a mathematical harmony.

By the time Frank crossed the Orlando city limits he had made his decision. He knew Mike would be in his office at this time of day. The lot was open on Saturday's but Frank stopped coming in five years ago to spend the weekends with Karen. The sales manager at the time threatened to fire him so Frank threatened to quit. Of course Mike had to step in to prevent a confrontation. Two weeks later Frank was shaking hands with the new manager. "Nice to meet you Peter," Frank said. "I'm Frank, and I'll see you Monday morning."

Frank found Mike sitting at his desk. "Hey Frank, how are you? What are you doing here on a Saturday?" Mike said, leaning back in his chair and interlocking his fingers behind his head.

"Mike, this isn't going to be easy for me, and I'm sorry for the way I'm doing this, but I won't be coming back to work, I'm retired as of yesterday," Frank said.

Mike leaned forward and slipped off his glasses. "Well, you know Frank, this doesn't surprise me. I kind of expected it after you told me you were buying a boat yesterday. We're really going to miss you around here, except for Nick."

"Nick quit a couple weeks ago," Frank interrupted "Tommy's the manager now."

"Oh yeah, Tommy, what a find he was," Mike said sarcastically. "Listen Frank, I'm not going to try and change your mind. I know you to well for that, and I hope everything works out the way you want it to. If it doesn't, you know you can come back to work here anytime you want."

"Thanks Mike, I appreciate that."

The two men gave one another a half hug; they had been friends a long time. Frank found some of the people he had worked with for years before he left. After a few

STRANGE WIND

good-byes and wishes of good luck Frank slipped out to his car.

    As he drove away from Tomasino's for the last time, he wondered what Karen would've thought. She'd only been gone a week and he had quit his job of nine years, and went from driving a Town Car to a clown car. Now he was about to move out of a nice, safe house onto a boat that he had been on for about an hour and all because of a song, a kid in a paper hat, and a tobacco-spitting mechanic.

CHAPTER 7

A duffel bag full of clothes, the Johnny Branson CDs and some other odds and ends lay next to the box of tools in the hatchback. The little car followed the same path back to Crystal River. Frank pulled into the marina and saw Wally sitting on the dock fishing. He unloaded the car and began carrying his cargo toward D-8.

"Where're you heading?" Wally asked with a string of drool hanging from his lip, disappearing into the water below the dock.

"Key West," Frank announced.

"It's because of the naked women ain't it?" Wally said watching the bobber tied to his fishing line as it floated on the water's surface.

Frank tossed the duffel bag onto the deck of the *Don't Worry*. "No I think it was the escaping the rat race part that got to me," Frank said, hoping that someday Wally could do the same. "I need to do something about my car though." He wondered if the mechanic, now turned fisherman, might have a suggestion.

"You see that old wooden trawler over there?" Wally pointed in the direction of an old fishing boat lying on its side near the fence.

"Yeah, I see it," said Frank.

"If you want to pull your car over there, it can sit there for as long as you want," Wally said, and then he spit into the water.

That's what Frank was hoping to hear.

Once the little car was backed in beside the old boat it was hard to spot. Frank locked it up and started back toward the dock. He had forty dollars in his hand by the time he reached Wally and offered it to him.

"Here, thanks for all your help."

Wally looked at the money but didn't take it; instead he turned back toward his bobber.

"Do me a favor," he said. "Take that money and buy yourself a drink at the first bar you see in the Keys, and then give the rest to the first nude gal you see running down the street. If it was my first night in Key West, that's exactly how I'd like to blow forty bucks." Frank folded the bills, and put them in his pocket with a smile.

"At least take the keys in case you need to move it," Frank said. Wally took the car keys and laid them in his tackle box. Frank waved good-bye as he boarded the *Don't Worry*. Wally just nodded and spit.

Frank navigated down the river and turned on the global positioning system. He located the owner's manual in the cabin and quickly read though it last night. After the short study session he felt pretty confident that he could use the navigational tool.

It was a beautiful day as he entered the Gulf of Mexico, around ten o'clock. The sun bounced off the blue waters as he pointed the bow of the yacht south. Reaching into the duffel he pulled out a five by seven picture of Karen and him. Using a couple of rubber bands he had brought, he strapped it to the center of the steering wheel. The picture was taken years ago while they stood in front of the bow rider. For some reason when he looked at the picture his mind didn't wander back to Karen but to Wally. Frank wondered if Wally ever had a wife or a relationship where minutes seemed like hours when you were apart, but they flew by like seconds when you were together. Maybe, he had a time where someone was his whole world and she dumped him for someone else. Frank thought about how much harder that would be than never finding that special person at all. Frank looked at the picture as Florida drifted by, three miles off his port side.

 Seventeen years and Karen was gone way too soon. Frank wondered how many people never found the person that could make them smile as they watched their first car being pulled out of a sinkhole by a wrecker. Or someone like Karen who brought tears of joy on his thirtieth birthday. When they drove out to the Ocala Forest and laid out a picnic lunch for him in her birthday suit. Karen could not be duplicated and they loved each other to the very end. Seventeen years was not long enough, but Frank figured most people never even have a second of what he and Karen had together.

 After a couple hours of cruising, Frank started to think about getting lunch and angled slightly toward shore. The *Don't Worry* was south of Tampa Bay as it closed in on the coastline. Frank had maintained a course where he could see the multi-storied hotels stretched along Florida's West Coast. Now as he came closer to the beaches he could see the people that must be residing in them beginning to gather up their beach towels, umbrellas, and coolers. Soon they would be checking out and heading for home to prepare for work Monday morning. Frank had no idea what Monday held for him. All he knew was he had broken free of the responsibility for anything other than himself. He also knew that Karen was probably looking down at him, shaking her head and laughing, wishing she were right beside him.

Frank came up on an inlet and figured that there would be at least one bar and grill not too far along its shores. He eased off the throttle and steered toward the inlet, and after passing under a drawbridge he was not disappointed. A sixteen-foot tall plywood alligator stood on its hind legs, smiling with a mug of beer in one hand. In the other one he held a red flag that read 'Gator Bait's Bar and Grill.' If you've lived in Florida for any amount of time you know two things. Wherever there's a mud hole big enough to get a boat in, someone will build a bar and grill on it. The other thing is, even though the alligator is considered one of the most terrifying animals in the wild, Floridians seemed to find them cute and cuddly. They also believed they have a charming sense of humor.

Frank found a place to dock his yacht next to the happy reptile. He switched off the engines and the sounds of hooting and hollering filled the warm Gulf coast air. Frank knew it could only mean one thing; it's Sunday afternoon and the Tampa Bay Buccaneers were on TV. Frank tied off the *Don't Worry* and walked along the pier toward the bar. The whole side of the Gator Bait was completely open, scattered with tables inside and out. Most of the tables were empty but not a seat could be found at the bar near the TV. Frank took a seat at the table that gave him the best glimpses of the game. It was in clear view when high fives, back slapping and the 'how the hell did that happen' body language wasn't going on. Finally, after years of how the hell did that happen, the high fives and backslapping were becoming more common. Frank knew all too well, since he had been a fan ever since Tampa was awarded the team in '76.

A woman, about Frank's age but looked as though she'd had a few pretty tough years approached Frank.

"What can I get for you dear?" she asked.

"I'll have a cheeseburger and whatever you have on tap," Frank said, not wanting to make her life any harder than it already was.

The Buccaneers were ahead by a touchdown when a commercial came on and the crowd relaxed.

"That your boat out there?" A happy go lucky fellow who was a little on the heavy side, spun around on his barstool and asked Frank.

"Yeah, I just got her a couple day ago up in Crystal River," Frank answered.

"I saw you pull up with her, she's a good looking boat. Where you heading? He asked.

"Key West," Frank answered.

"Oh yeah, I hear there's a lot of them drag queens down there," the man said.

A little guy next to him swung around still holding on to his mug of beer and spoke. "That's men that dress like women, ain't it?" he said, looking at his bar buddy.

"Yeah, the men dress up like women and the women don't wear nothing," the friend answered and they both laughed.

The two men wished Frank good luck and went back to watching the game. It seemed the 'nude girls running around Key West' fantasy was covering the state pretty thoroughly.

The waitress set Frank's beer and burger on the table.

"Enjoy," she said.

"Thank you," Frank began eating while trying to keep an eye on the game.

A man from the bar that Frank had not noticed made his way over to him.

"Excuse me," he said. "I'm sorry to bother you while you're having your lunch, but I over heard you say that you're heading to Key West. Is that right?" He pulled out a chair from the table next to Frank's and sat down.

"Yeah, I hope to be there by nightfall," Frank answered followed with a bite of cheeseburger.

"How long you plan on staying?" the man asked.

"I honestly have no idea," Frank said as he took a swallow of beer, thinking he was about to hear another nude-girl-running-down-the-street story.

"I'm in the jewelry business here in St. Petersburg. I have a friend in Key West who owns a pawn shop," the man began. "He's got some connection over in the Bahamas, Bimini I think it is where he sends a lot of gold trinkets and chains. People will go to Key West and generally decide to stay longer than they planned, so they end up pawning some jewelry to finance their extended stay, you see?"

Frank didn't know why the guy was telling him this, but he saw how that could happen.

"Don, my friend sends the stuff to a gift shop on Bimini, or wherever the hell it is, and they put it in little cardboard boxes that say "Bahama Gold" on them. Tourists come over and buy them up as fast as they can get them in the boxes, as a souvenir from the Bahamas. Someone may fly over to the Bahamas for vacation and buy a bracelet. Then, a year or two later the drive down to the Key's for a week-end get-away. They end up pawning it to my friend so they can stay an extra night. Pretty soon it gets shipped right back to where they bought it." As the man talked he used a lot of hand gestures.

"Interesting business," Frank said between bites of cheeseburger, not sure why this guy was telling him all this.

"I have some things I've taken in on trade that I was going to drive down to him later this week," he went on, "it would save me a full day of driving if you could take it down there for me."

"Sorry, but I'm not interested," Frank said somewhat

suspicious of the odd request.

"Look it's just a small box with some cheap gold-plated chains and stuff in it, and I'll give you a hundred dollars if you could help me out here."

The years of making deals as a car salesman got the better of him. "I'll have to see the stuff first, because I'm not going to smuggle any drugs or any thing like that," Frank said. "And if everything looks okay and you take care of my tab here you got yourself a deal."

The man looked at Frank's lunch; figuring ten dollars would cover the tip and all.

"Great, I'll go get the box," the man said and went out the front door to the parking lot, while Frank finished his lunch. Frank was wiping his mouth with a napkin when the man returned with a clear plastic box slightly bigger than a shoebox. Frank thought it looked innocent enough. He sat the box on the table in front of Frank. Frank leaned forward and pulled the vacuum-sealed lid off and picked up a handful of gold necklaces, bracelets, rings and charms all tangled together in one big glob. The man held up some bills in his hand as he waited for Frank to take them. A ten-dollar bill was already laying on the table for the waitress.

"You've got to be kidding me!" Frank said, holding the ball of gold plated accessories, hanging between his fingers like a handful of spaghetti.

The man shrugged his shoulders. "Tourist," he said. "Here's the address."

Frank dropped the golden glob back into the box. "What the hell!" he thought. Taking the address and the money, he picked up the box and headed for his boat.

"I'll call Don tonight and let him know that you'll be there tomorrow," the man said, as Frank left.

Back out on the open sea, with a full stomach and a hundred dollars richer, Frank continued his trip south.

Next stop would be his new home. Key West would be a place where nothing would remind him of his loss, and a place where he could start his life over. If things worked out like he hopes they would, he would return to Orlando in a few months and list the house with a real estate agent, then return to Key West forever. The *Don't Worry* was running in top form and Frank was finally thinking about what lay ahead of him. Life on and island sounded so relaxing, just him and his boat. No more having to try and talk someone into buying a car in slacks and a tie in the Florida heat. Trying to meet every request they had, just to find out they had a bankruptcy they somehow forgot to mention. They wouldn't have been able to buy a ten year old car from a buy-here pay-here lot.

    No grass to mow, no house to paint, and if he didn't like the neighbors he could just pull up anchor and move on. Hell maybe the girls did go nude at night, he didn't know. If he had all the answers before he left Orlando it wouldn't be much of an adventure, and he might as well have stayed home.

    Sooner than expected Florida, wasn't beside him anymore. He could see Highway A1A jumping from one island to the next. Frank Summers was in the Florida Keys.

CHAPTER 8

The sun was setting as Highway A1A ended and the island of Key West sat in full view of Frank as the lazy nightlife on a Sunday evening was just beginning to stir. Frank shut down the engines as the *Don't Worry* settled into the Gulf coast waters. He slipped the anchor over the side and sat and watched as the sun disappeared into the ocean. Frank quietly listened from his boat to the sounds of a band playing somewhere off in the distance.

That somewhere was Captain Crabbies a favorite hangout of the Key West locals.

****

"For a three piece band they're pretty good aren't they?" Madeline the bartender was saying. A local businessman sat at the bar slowly stirring his margarita. "Donny, did you hear me?" She said, while sticking two dollars in the tip jar, left on the bar by a couple on vacation from Minnesota.

"What the hell is wrong with you Donny?" she asked.

The man stopped stirring the cocktail and took a drink of the cold margarita.

"You know Dean, that guy from New Orleans that was working for me?" Don took a long slow drink from his glass.

"Yeah, I know that nut." Madeline was not thrilled by the mention of his name. He would come into the bar acting like some sort of a big shot and never tip a nickel.

"He took his boat and went back to New Orleans yesterday." Don said.

"Good, I never cared for that cheap little bastard anyway," said the red-headed bartender. "He was always rude and he never tipped." She wiped down the areas where the Northerners had left their empty glasses.

"No, not good, now I don't have anyone to make my jewelry runs to Bimini." Don was a man in his early fifties, hair beginning to thin, and belly starting to overlap his belt. He had been in Key West for over twenty-five years and loved ever minute of it.

"So why don't you just quit? You can't be making that much money off selling crappy jewelry." Madeline was standing directly across the bar from him. She had one hand on her large hip and a towel hanging from the other.

"Quit, yeah right, I could just quit." Don repeated the words like Madeline didn't know what she was talking about.

"Well, do whatever you want for all I care," she tossed the rag onto one of the coolers under the bar. Opening the one next to it, she took out three bottles of Budweiser and twisted off the caps. Madeline carried them around the bar to some college boys seated at a table near the stage. They were hoping to find some Key West cuties before the night was over.

****

From his boat Frank was able to recognize the song the

band in the distance was playing. "Surfs up at Sundown" was a Johnny Branson tune. It was peaceful as he pulled a bottle of whiskey from the duffel bag sitting next to the box of soon to be Bahama gold. Frank decided he would spend the night with his yacht anchored right where it was. The marina offices would probable be closed, and he wouldn't want to dock anywhere he wasn't suppose to. Since he was going to be living aboard it really didn't matter where it was.

He brought a pack of cheese crackers and a bag of corn chips from Orlando which would get him by for tonight he thought. After he found a place to dock the next morning he would stock up on groceries.

****

The band at Captain Crabbies was still playing a few hours later as the somewhat intoxicated Frank put the top back on the near empty bottle of Jack Daniel's. He moved slowly down into the cabin of the yacht. Drinking as much as he did was not a good idea. It caused him to be very vulnerable to the memories of Karen. The rocking of the boat did not work to his advantage either. Due to the alcohol, a rocking boat, and missing his wife it was not an easy night.

Frank slept later than he had wanted to the next morning and he was feeling down for not getting the day started sooner. He had lost control of himself last night and resolved to focus on his future in Key West. It was going to be the only way he could make it though these difficult times. After being together for so long, and to be separated so suddenly, would be hard on anyone. He also vowed that drinking to excess was not the answer. Frank pulled up the anchor and climbed the ladder to the bridge.

He sat at the helm for a few minutes and looked across the blue water at the island of Key West. The bright sun was warm against his face and squeaking seagulls had replaced the sounds of last night's band. Key West seemed to be inviting him to come ashore. It was the place for him to be right now. Frank guided his boat toward the island and cruised along its shoreline, passing by several marinas that were big and congested. After entering a horseshoe shaped cove he came across a little marina that seemed more like what he had in mind when he left Orlando.

Key Coast Marina sat protected from the open ocean with its faded wooden sign hanging over the water in front of the office. Finding an empty spot near the gas pump he tied off his new home and went to see what he could find out about permanent residency. Frank entered the marina and rang the silver bell sitting on the counter. A man who barely looked old enough to drink came out of the small office area.

"Hi my name is Doug. How can I help you?" he asked. He was wearing red shorts, a white polo shirt, and boat shoes with no socks. He in no way tried to hide the fact that he was fond of the same sex.

"Well I'm looking for a place to dock my boat long-term and was wondering if you had anything available." Hoping the phrase docking his boat long-term didn't have a hidden homosexual meaning he was not aware of.

"How long is it?" the young man asked.

"What? Oh, um the boat, it's a thirty-two footer," Frank felt like the biggest jerk in the world. Doug pulled a folder out from under the counter, somewhat afraid to take his eyes off Frank. This is just great, in Key West less then five minutes and I already offended the first person I've met, Frank thought.

"Are you going to live aboard?" Doug asked.

"Yes, I plan on staying on the boat," Frank answered.

"Okay, let me see, yes we have a spot available. You can pay for a month at a time and stay as long as you would like," Doug said, as he looked at a page in the folder.

"That would be great," Frank said reaching for his wallet. Papers were signed, money was exchanged, and Doug showed Frank which slip he had just rented.

Frank guided the *Don't Worry* away from the gas pump and into its new home. After securing the lines to the dock, and hooking up to the marina's electric source, he headed down below to take a shower.

Dressed in clean shorts and one of his favorite Hawaiian style shirts, it was time to get a bite to eat and deliver the plastic container to the address as he had promised. A small cafe situated next to the marina had just opened. Frank took a set near the window.

"Would you like something to drink?" The young waitress asked as she handed him a menu.

"Coffee please," Frank said returning the smile and opening the menu. He had an omelet and toast as he watched out the window, a half a dozen seagulls scoured the parking lot for bits of food in the morning sunshine. Frank finished his coffee and took his check over to the cash register.

"Can you tell me how to get to Don's pawnshop?" he asked as he paid for his breakfast. The young woman behind the cash register began pointing different directions and naming off landmarks and street names. Frank thanked her and headed off toward Duval Street. The pawnshop was farther than Frank had expected it to be. On foot in the morning heat the island town seemed pretty big. Finally coming to the cross street he was looking for he saw the little storefront with "Don Gold and Pawn" painted on the window. The name was a play on words from the movie 'On Golden Pond' Frank figured.

STRANGE WIND

A bell tied to the inside of the door by a piece of string jingled as Frank opened it and the cool air-conditioned air rushed out to meet him. It felt especially good after the long hot walk. A short man, a little overweight and balding was bent over with the crack of his ass showing. He was slapping the side of a television set just inside the door. A picture of a weatherman that looked like he was standing in front of one of those funhouse mirrors was on the screen.

"Come on, you piece of junk you were working fine yesterday," the man was saying, talking to the television when Frank entered.

"Good morning, are you Don?" Frank said to the ass crack.

"Yeah, I'm Don who wants to know?" the man said while still abusing the television.

"My name is Frank and I've got a package here for you."

The man stood up and reached out his hand to take the package while still looking at the television. Frank handed the box to Don and walked over to where a bicycle was leaning against some assorted golfing equipment.

"Where did you say this came from?" the man said still holding the box in the same position that Frank had handed it to him.

"I didn't get the guy's name, he said he was a friend of yours," Frank answered, now realizing how strange it seemed that the man hadn't given his name.

"I met him in a bar south of Tampa. I think he said he owned a jewelry store in St. Petersburg. He overheard me saying I was on my way to Key West, and asked if I would bring that down here for him. How much do you want for the bicycle?"

"Was he driving a BMW? Thirty dollars," Don answered.

"I'm not sure. I came by boat and never saw the parking lot. I'll give you twenty for it," Frank countered.

"You came here by boat. When did you get in?" Don asked, forgetting to negotiate on the bike.

"I just pulled into the marina this morning," Frank said turning his attention away from the bike wondering what was with all the questions.

"What kind of boat do you have?" Don peeled the plastic lid off the container to get a peek inside.

"It's a thirty-two foot cabin cruiser. How about I give you twenty bucks for the bike?" Frank asked again not wanting to walk back.

"Yeah, yeah, sure whatever, have you ever been to Bimini?" Don said blowing off the deal on the bicycle, he was more interested in the boat.

"No, I think I came up Front Street from the marina, then down Duval and then whatever you call this street. Those are the only places I've been." Frank pulled a small stack of twenties out of his pocket, seven to be exact.

"No, no, no it's not a street, it's an island in the Bahamas," Don said. Damn it Frank knew that, he blamed his not knowing on the desire to own the bicycle and not having to walk back.

"Oh yeah, no, no I've never been there but I know where you're talking about."

"Listen this package you brought here, did Robert tell you why I needed it?" Don asked, referring to the plastic box.

"Yeah, I think he said you ship it to the Bahamas and they sell it to tourists or something like that. Is there a tax on used bicycles?" Frank said, knowing that there was but being a car salesman for so long he knew all the tricks to try to save a dime. Not that he needed to, he just liked to play the game. Playing dumb about taxes could sometimes get them to take care of Uncle Sam themselves.

"What, oh, the bike, um no, no it's just twenty bucks. Listen, I had a guy running the stuff over there for me, but he went back to New Orleans. If you want to pick up some extra money, since you just moved down here, maybe we could work something out," Don said; putting the twenty Frank handed him in his pocket without even looking at it. He sat the box down on top of the blurred television.

"Who said I moved down here?" Frank asked suspiciously.

"Tourists don't usually come to Key West and buy used bicycles" Don answered, shrugging his shoulders. Frank had now met two people in Key West and managed to embarrass himself both times.

"I didn't come down here looking for a job. I came here to get away from all that," Frank said, holding on to the handlebars of the bike.

"Look, I can see where you're coming from," Don said, "but you can only watch the sun go down once a day. After a few weeks, once you've visited all the bars, restaurants, and done the tourist crap, you're going to wish you had something to do. Now there's no sense of thinking of this offer as a job, it's just you and your boat cruising to Bimini twice a week."

"Twice a week, huh?" Frank said. What Don was saying made some sense. "How much does it pay?" Frank asked.

"I was paying the other guy before two-hundred a trip, but if you could start by making a run later today I'll pay you two-hundred-and-fifty bucks." Frank began to calculate, a hundred a trip should cover his expenses for fuel and stuff and it would only take a few hours each trip, plus he had learned yesterday that cruising in your own boat was quite enjoyable.

"What time today?" Frank asked. Don looked at his watch.

"How about twelve o'clock. You can pick up the gold here at twelve."

"Okay," Frank said. "I'll see you at twelve o'clock."

CHAPTER 9

Frank peddled his way back to the marina. Down in the cabin of the *Don't Worry* he looked over some charts that the Harris's had left behind. They probably would have been taken out and thrown them away if the trade hadn't been made so quickly. There were even dishes in the cabinets and towels in the head, which made things easier for Frank. Once again he studied the book on the global positioning system. On the way down from Crystal River he never lost sight of land, but a trip to Bimini would be a little more difficult. After convincing himself he knew what he was doing, he rode into town to stock up on groceries.

****

Back at the boat, with everything he had bought put away, he had a light lunch consisting of a ham sandwich, some chips and a soda. Frank got on his bike and noticed two men sitting in a pickup truck with a magnetic sign on the door that read "Magic Wizard Boat Repair". Frank waved hello to the men, thinking he should keep them in mind since he's going to be using his boat more often. The two men did not return the greeting, they only stared at him as he peddled past. "Not very friendly," Frank thought as he turned onto Duval Street. He parked his bicycle outside of Don's pawnshop.

"Hey great, there you are! I got a hold of Dorrey; he's the jeweler over in Alice Town on Bimini. This is where you'll dock," Don said, folding out a map of the Caribbean Island. "Atlantic Marina is on this side of the island," pointing to the map, and writing a three-digit number on it with a felt tip marker.

"This is the slip number that Dorrey rents for you to dock at," Don said, drawing a line along the roads of Alice Town. Don showed Frank how to get to Dorrey's jewelry shop. Don disappeared into the back room of the store as Frank looked over the map. When he came back he was carrying a large, black, hard-sided suitcase.

"Whoa! Wait a minute! That's what you want me to deliver. I thought it was that little box I brought to you this morning. What's going on here?" Frank said, having second thoughts about the whole thing.

"Well it's what you brought me along with some other stuff I've taken in on trade this week," Don answered.

Don laid the suitcase down on its side on the floor. He released the latches and opened the case in front of the television that was now turned off. It was full of gold chains, rings, money clips and several other gold plated odds and ends. Frank raked his fingers through the contents; sure he would come across bags of cocaine or at least marijuana, but there was nothing but cheap jewelry. He ran his hand along the lining of the suitcase, and the lid, but no hidden compartments could be found.

"Are you okay?" Don asked Frank. He was still on his knees digging though the suitcase, trying to find the illegal drugs. He wanted to back out of the arrangement before getting busted in a foreign country, someplace where they do, no telling what to prisoners. Key West jail would probably be no better. Frank had to stop; his mind was out of control. It was just a suitcase full of gold that one honest businessman was trying to deliver to another one.

"You're single, aren't you?" Don said, watching Frank sweating on the floor.

"I'm sorry. What did you say?" Frank had no idea what the man was saying, but the sound of Don's voice brought him back to reality.

"You got a girlfriend?" Don asked, reaching down to help Frank to his feet.

"Do I have a what, a girlfriend, no, no I don't, I just got out of a long relationship." Not wanting sympathy from the shopkeeper Frank chose not to tell him his wife had passed away.

"Oh I see," Don said, slowly bending down to close up the suitcase. "Key West can be a very romantic place after the sun goes down."

Frank stepped back. What the hell was this conversation about?

"Don't you worry my friend," Don smiled. "When you get back from Bimini we'll get you a girlfriend. From now on anything you need, you let me know and I'll take care of it. What marina is your boat docked at?" Don placed a hand on Frank's shoulder

"My boat, it's at Key Coast," Frank said.

"Oh Key Coast Marina, that's Paul and Ruby's place," Don said as the two men walked toward the door together, Frank carrying the heavy suitcase.

"Have you met Paul? His wife runs the cafe next door. Nice people, but their son Doug." Don shook his head.

"If you see him come in late at night with a girl on his arm, and they start making out down on the pier, like I hear they sometimes do, you may not want to watch that for very long. Come by tomorrow and I'll pay you for your trip okay?"

"Okay Don, I'll see you tomorrow." Frank took the suitcase and left the pawnshop.

He was convinced, once again, that everything was on the level as he strapped the suitcase to the bike and began peddling along Duval Street.

Frank noticed a woman walking down the sidewalk going in the same direction. What had Don been saying, something about a girlfriend? Of course it was too early for that, but Frank's eyes were sure glued to the pink fabric of the tight little mini skirt that stretched across the backside of the pedestrian. Just as he passed her the light turned red and he brought his bike to a stop. Looking to his right out of the corner of his eye, he could see her catching up with him. It was too early for a relationship, but a little conversation, maybe dinner together later tonight after he returned from his trip might be nice. Don said Key West was for romance or something like that. Frank wasn't exactly sure what he had said. It was during the period when Frank was determined to prove Don as some sort of drug smuggler. Frank sat on his bike with one foot on the ground watching the traffic crossing in front of him. She was standing right beside him now waiting for the light to change. He tugged at the collar of his shirt as if to get a little cool air stirring and thought he saw her smiling out of the corner of his eye. The perfect opening, make a comment about the heat he thought. As he was about to make the "Boy it's sure hot out, isn't it" icebreaker, a pickup truck full of teen-age boys whizzed across in front of them.

"Hail to the queen!" one of the boys in the back of the truck hollered as they passed. The woman shot them the finger. That's when Frank saw that her arms were almost twice the size of his. At forty-two years old he almost pissed his pants. The light could not turn green fast enough, he decided to keep his eyes on the road the rest of the way back to the boat.

CHAPTER 10

    Frank lifted the bike onto the boat and set the suitcase down on the deck. While storing away his bike, the suitcase fell over on its side. Frank used a couple of bungee cords to hold the bike in place and turned back to the black piece of luggage. He lifted it off the deck to carry it down into the cabin. The side that rested against the deck was covered with a white powder residue. Frank wiped his hand along the imitation leather, then lifted it to his nose. It was fiberglass dust, from the floor of the boat. Mr. and Mrs. Harris must have had some work done recently to the deck of the *Don't Worry*. He was surprised that he hadn't seen it before now, but figured that's what he got for not inspecting it before closing the deal. Frank took the suitcase down the steps, almost falling on the first one, but regaining his balance and placing it on the cabin's floor. Frank then hopped off the *Don't Worry,* untied her, and went up to the bridge. The little yacht almost started before he turned the key. It didn't take much cranking power to get her going, which pleased Frank. He turned on the global positioning system and headed out to sea.
    Soon Key West disappeared behind him. Frank felt a

little eerie with no land in sight, but was not worried. Everything seemed to be in order according to the instruments on the dash. It wasn't long before land appeared on the horizon. Bimini Island was right where it was supposed to be according to the charts. Frank pulled out the map Don had given him; he spotted his first landmark, an old lighthouse. Frank headed his boat to the left of it to where the marina was located. "Simple as pie," Frank thought to himself as he docked in the appropriate slip.

Untying his bike and setting it ashore, Frank retrieved the suitcase from the cabin. He took a quick glance at the map, folded it up and put it in his shirt pocket, and made his way toward the jeweler's shop. The sun was hot as he rode along, but the slow speed of the bicycle provided a nice breeze. He had to slow down several times as he rode past the small storefronts, making sure he didn't pass his destination. Just as he was about to turn around, thinking he had gone too far, he saw a sign on the left advertising Bahama Gold the number one souvenir of the Caribbean. Frank laughed to himself as he thought of the strange circle some of the gold would travel. He parked his bike outside on the sidewalk and started inside. The jeweler was apparently watching as he pulled up.

"No! No! No!" the man cried as he came around the counter, toward Frank, but ran right past him. Rushing out the door he came back in pushing Frank's bike.

"No leave bike outside or it goes bye-bye."

"Oh thank you very much. I should have known better," Frank said. "You must be Dorrey."

"Yes, I am," Dorrey said, looking at Frank with suspicion. "Don called and told me he had a new man coming today. Very good, how was your trip? No problems I hope."

"No, no, everything was fine," Frank answered.

"Good, let me see what you have brought for me today," Dorrey said as he took the case to the counter and opened it. Frank looked inside the glass cases along the walls and saw the gold chains in the Bahama Gold boxes and laughed to himself. Dorrey went through the suitcase of merchandise. It took him longer than Frank had expected, nearly a half an hour. He finally turned to Frank.

"This all looks very good. You tell Don thank you very much, and give this to him please." He handed Frank a thick envelope. Frank took what appeared to be an envelope full of cash. Don hadn't said anything about an envelope, but Frank took it and stuck it in his shirt pocket.

"Okay then, I guess I'll see you later," Frank said as he took his bike and the empty suitcase back outside. He peddled his way back to the *Don't Worry.*

It wasn't long before he was pulling back into the slip at Key Coast feeling pretty good about his first over seas voyage. Frank showered and changed his clothes and decided to look around the town a little. The sun was just starting to set on a beautiful Key West night. He left his bike behind and followed the music and laughter that led him to Mallory Square. There he watched as street performers put on their shows for the tourists, followed by the passing of the hat. Frank watched a man squeeze himself into an orange crate, then had a volunteer hold a tiny hoop, which he dove through without even touching. He laughed at the man with a little dog who could do all sorts of funny stunts. As he made his way around the square he stopped at a seafood restaurant and sat down at an outside table. Frank ordered a shrimp and scallop dinner and leaned back to enjoy the carnival type atmosphere. The food was good. A crowd of people from the cruise ship in port for the evening were enjoying a night that doesn't seem to exist in the everyday world. It seemed like a world away from bosses, traffic on Interstate

4 and trying to get by and pay the bills. They watched a shirtless man with hair down to his waist, as he lit up the dark sky with three flaming torches. One by one he tilted his head back and dramatically placed the fire down his throat. Frank enjoyed the large plate of seafood while a trio of steel drum entertainers displayed their talent nearby filling the warm tropical air with a sound that can only mean you're on an island. This is a vacation of a lifetime to many of the people in the crowd, a night they'll never forget.

For Frank it was a trip back to the night when he had first met Karen. The sights and sounds of a state fair, that comes around once a year is an every night thing at Mallory Square. Frank downed the last of his frozen rumrunner as he looked up into the night sky. He talked directly to his lost love.

"I'm in Key West without you honey, I miss you." Frank paid his tab and headed up Duval Street. The sounds and feel in the air were therapeutic to his mind. He felt as if he belonged here in some odd way. A couple that seemed to be about his age walked by, holding each other closer than necessary in the Florida heat. Frank thought the sight of such a display of affection would have killed him a few days ago, and in Orlando it might have, but here in Key West something was different. It almost seemed like the island was calling to him, that if he couldn't have Karen then this is where he needed to be.

Frank walked past an open-air bar that looked like they couldn't close if they wanted to. Frank remembered the promise he had made to Wally about buying a drink at the first bar he came to, and giving the rest of the money to an exhibitionist. He didn't know if this was the first bar he had passed or not, because he hadn't been paying attention. It was the first bar since he remembered the promise. Not that Wally would ever know or care for that matter.

There didn't appear to be any female streakers out, or at least not yet. Frank went in and had a seat at the bar next to a guy who looked like he had retired to the Keys many years ago, and spent most of that time in the bars. There was one man on a small stage with a guitar and no shoes, who seemed to be able to play every song ever written, and was pretty damn good at it too.

"What will it be pal?" A fat man wearing a T-shirt with the sleeves cut off stood across the dark wooden bar from him. Frank started to order a Rum Runner since he'd just had one at the restaurant, but figured since it was really Wally's money he was spending he would order what he thought Wally would order. Frank thought for a second then smiled.

"Just give me a bottle of Budweiser," he answered. The bartender set a cardboard drink coaster in front of him and went after the beer. Frank picked up the coaster; a picture of a deserted island with a single palm tree was printed in the center. "The Island Breeze Bar," was spelled out around the outer edge. After the beer was delivered he took a long drink then he swiveled around on his barstool to face the band, if you can call one guy with a guitar standing on a small stage a band.

A couple of women who looked to be in their early thirties were seated at one of the small tables. They were drinking drinks that looked like something out of a cartoon they were so bright in color. The first woman had her back to Frank. She was wearing a form-fitting red dress. He watched as she dangled her shoe off of the heel of her foot to the beat of the music. Frank took another swig of his beer and was really enjoying the man on stage.

The man would sing a song to perfection and then make fun of how bad he sounded. Frank finished his beer and as he turned to call for the bartender, he noticed the other woman at the table looking at him and whispering to

her friend. She had short brown hair that framed her cute face. The blonde turned and looked at Frank then quickly swung her head back toward her friend. He gave a little nod and a smile her way not wanting to be rude. She tilted her head and smiled back. After listening to a couple more songs the two ladies finished their drinks and got up to leave. The one that had been facing Frank walked directly toward him. She was wearing a black mini-skirt and a white blouse that didn't leave much to the imagination.
"Hi, my name is Rhonda," she said, "I'm on vacation from Jacksonville. How about you?"
"Orlando." Frank answered.
"Oh really, I have a friend that lives in Winter Springs. That's near there isn't it?" she said flipping back her hair with a toss of her head.
"It's practically part of Orlando." Frank smiled.
"I'm going to be here until Friday. If you'd like to get together for a drink or something here's my number at the hotel, give me a call."
Before Frank could pick his jaw up out of his lap, she was gone. Frank looked at the napkin she had pressed into his hand. He unfolded it as the old man on the bar stool next to him looked at him as if he had just walked on water. Her name and a phone number were neatly printed in blue ink. No hotel name or room number, very classy. She'd like for you to call but don't think you're just going to have sex with her. The kind of woman Frank could fall for, very sexy, with class. Frank looked at the napkin as the older gentleman lit up a cigarette and laid his lighter down on the bar. Frank carefully refolded the napkin. He held it to his nose and drew in the smell of the perfumed fragrance that was lingering from Rhonda's touch. He picked up the lighter and lit the corner of it, as it burned down near his fingers he laid it in the ashtray sitting on the bar. Frank bought the man a drink while paying for his

own, and made his way back to the *Don't Worry*. He'd had enough excitement for one night.

****

The waves were gently lapping against the hull of the *Don't Worry* as Frank woke the next morning after a good night's sleep. He started a pot of coffee and walked over to the cafe next to the marina. Frank fished some change out of his pocket, bought a newspaper from the paper box out front and went back to his boat. He poured himself some coffee and sat down on the deck. After a relaxing couple of hours, Frank rode his bike over to Don's pawnshop.

A woman was standing next to Don as Frank entered.

"Its got great color, and the picture is really sharp," Don was telling her with one hand resting on the television that was a piece of junk yesterday, but was the best buy on the island today. Don saw Frank and gave him a nod to let him know he would be just a minute. Frank held up a hand, giving Don the "I'm in no hurry" gesture as he began to look around the shop. After making his way up one aisle and down another he came across a large rack of CDs. They were arranged in alphabetical order according to the artist's name so it didn't take long to come across the Johnny Branson selections. Frank pulled one from the rack. It was one he had not seen yet. On the cover was the smiling musician on a barstool with his back to a tiki bar. He was in shorts and a Hawaiian shirt with a straw hat sitting side ways on his head. Two young ladies in bathing suits were standing on either side of him feeding him strawberries. "I'm Not Where I Thought I Was," was the title. Frank pulled out the other two CD's of Branson's and looked at them. One he already had and the other showed Johnny riding an alligator while chasing a dozen or so bikini-clad females down a sandy beach. It was titled "Sand Between My Toes." Frank looked at some of the song titles and smiled. He really didn't know anything about the singer. Was he married? How did he break into the music business? He really didn't want to, afraid he might find out the guy couldn't even point out Florida on a map, or that he had never seen the ocean. Frank only knew that he really enjoyed the music. Like Bill said back at the Orlando sub shop the music was the spark that had got him to the Keys. Frank put the CD he already owned back on the rack and walked over to the other side of the shop where some stereos and video equipment was. He hadn't been able to play his CDs since he'd left Crystal River because there was no CD player on the boat. Don was still busy trying to sell the television to the woman. Frank found a small portable stereo with a CD player that looked as though it was still in good shape. He picked it up and carried it to the counter. Don was saying good-bye to the woman as she walked out the door

"Yes, bring your husband by later, but don't wait too long or someone else might buy it," Don called out after her. Frank handed the envelope from Dorrey to Don. He opened it and took out what looked to be seven or eight hundred dollars.

"Did you find it okay?" Don asked.

"Yeah, no problem, I was able to go right to it," Frank said. Don looked at the three items Frank set on the counter.

"Twenty bucks?" he said, looking at Frank almost as if it were a question seeing if Frank would haggle over a price that was already a good deal. Frank nodded his head and Don counted out two hundred and thirty dollars from the envelope and gave it to Frank.

"Has Madeline been by to see you yet?"

"Who?" Frank asked, looking puzzled.

"Oh, umm nothing, never mind," Don was backpedaling.

"Madeline, who's Madeline?"

"What, did I say Madeline, noooo. I said, how-ya-doin'" Don said, slurring the last three words together. Frank frowned

"Who is Madeline?" he asked again, now not sure if he heard Don right.

"Listen I'll need you to make another run Thursday at noon if that's alright with you," Don said trying to change the subject. Frank didn't fight him on this much since he really didn't know what the hell they were talking about.

"Yeah, I can make another run on Thursday no problem."

CHAPTER 11

Frank strapped the stereo and CDs to the rack on the back of his bike and rode back down Duval Street toward the marina. He parked the bike and found a place to plug in his used stereo. Frank put one of the new CDs in, and waited to see if the thing even played. Soon a song called *"Wind in my Sails"* came drifting out of the speakers. Johnny Branson had not disappointed Frank. The music was smoothing and laid-back, just like the songs he had heard before. Frank listened to his new stereo for a few moments then went down to the galley and brought up a loaf of bread, lunchmeat, mayonnaise, cheese and a beer and placed it on the little table that was up on the deck. He had gone back down the hatch to retrieve a knife and a plate when he heard a voice coming from the pier calling out his name. Frank grabbed the knife and plate and headed back up the cabin steps. He stumbled on the top one and dropped the knife onto the deck. A woman had just walked past his boat on the pier as he bent over to pick it up,

"Frank?" the woman called out again, walking in the opposite direction.

"I'm Frank," he called out as he wiped the knife off on

his shorts.

"Oh, there you are," she said as she turned around. She was wide and tall; she looked heavy but moved with a certain grace. Her white Capri pants were straining to hold it all together and the blue spaghetti-strap top didn't have a chance. Her hair was red and big and in perfect form.

"I've been looking all over for you," she smiled, as she stood at the edge of the dock beside Frank's boat.

"Um, I'm sorry, can I help you aboard?" Frank answered in a tone he hoped would convey he didn't know who she was.

"No that's alright, I can do it," she said, stepping into the deck of the boat with ease as the *Don't Worry* sank deeper into the Gulf Coast waters.

"I'm Madeline," she announced like Frank was supposed to know who she was by her name. She stood in front of him smiling like she was waiting for his approval of her. She was at least three inches taller than Frank who was 5' 10" himself. With her hair and the three-inch blue high heels she wore made her seem a foot taller. Her breasts were big, her thighs were big, her ass was big. Everything about this woman was big, but she didn't seem overweight. Everything was in proportion to everything else. Her body was the perfect shape that a guy would find attractive. It was just bigger.

"Don didn't tell you I was coming by did he?" she asked, her smile fading and a bit of a whine coming through in her voice. Frank felt uncomfortable; this huge person was hurt by him not knowing who she was.

"I'm sorry, but no one said anything to me about a visitor stopping by today," Frank answered. She hung her head slightly, a moment ago she was cheery and happy, and now she felt like someone had tried to make a fool of her.

"I'm sorry too," she said, with her head down she

reached for the rail to exit the boat.

"Wait a minute, you don't have to go," Frank blurted out, not sure why. Madeline stopped.

"Don said you and I would hit it off and that I should come down here and see you." Her body faced Frank's direction but her head faced the open waters. "I thought you and him had talked it over about me coming by to see you. People play tricks on me all the time where I work but I didn't think this was one of them. I'm so sorry I bothered you." She turned away from him. Frank thought she was going to cry.

"Look, you're not bothering me. I was just about to have a sandwich, would you like to join me?" he asked.

"No thank you, I'll just go back home until its time for me to go to work." she said.

"You're already here, and I've got the sandwich stuff already on the table. Would you like a beer or a Coke?" Frank said feeling sorry for the woman who was really very attractive.

"I don't drink before I go to work," she said.

"Fine, then I'll get you a Coke," Frank said, and disappeared into the cabin not knowing if she would be there when he came out or not. He felt the boat gently rock while getting the drink and a glass of ice. She'd either left or sat down. When Frank came out with of the companionway, he saw Madeline was spreading mayonnaise on four pieces of bread. Frank opened the Coke for his guest and poured it into the glass, he sat it in front of the lady. She put the one plate in the middle of the small table with the two sandwiches on it. Frank took one of the sandwiches.

"So where do you work?" he asked, sitting down in the chair across from her.

"I'm a bartender at Captain Crabbies on Simonton Street. It's more of a local's bar than the ones on Duval," she said while sipping her drink. "How long have you been in town?"

"I just got down here yesterday," Frank said, "how about you."

"I've been here since '92. Are you planning on staying long?" asked Madeline.

"Right now I don't plan on ever leaving, but I guess you never know what might happen." Frank took a bite of his sandwich. They visited until about one thirty then Madeline had to go. Her shift at Captain Crabbies started at two o'clock.

"It was sure nice meeting you. I'm glad you decided to stay for lunch," Frank said.

"I am too," she answered. "If you're not doing anything tonight, stop by Captain Crabbies and I'll buy you a drink." Frank said he might and watched her get into her little Ford Escort. Frank found it quite amazing the way her large body effortlessly fit into the small car. She backed out of the parking spot, gave a smile and waved Frank's way, and disappeared down the street. He liked her once she had calmed down to her normal self. She seemed warm and intelligent, with a good sense of humor, but boy was she big.

Frank decided to hit a few of the tourist attractions. He walked over to Mallory Square where he caught the Conch Train that took him on a tour of the island. It went by the Hemmingway House; Key West Cemetery, Southernmost Point and several other points of interest as the driver gave informative facts about the city. Frank was dropped off back at Mallory Square where he took in the Shipwreck Museum and walked the sponge market. Back on the *Don't Worry* he made himself dinner then sat out on the deck enjoying the ocean breeze with his newest CDs and a glass of whiskey and Coke. As the music ended Frank walked up to the marina and along the sea wall aimlessly.

STRANGE WIND

Then he crossed the parking lot heading back to his boat. A pink cab, normally yellow anywhere else but pink in Key West, had just dropped someone off, it slowed as it approached Frank.

"Can I give you a lift somewhere pal?" The cab driver spoke through the open window.

"No thanks, I got nowhere to go," Frank said, but before the driver could pull away he changed his mind.

"Hey wait a second, how about a lift to Captain Crabbies?"

CHAPTER 12

Madeline had her hands full with a busy crowd that night at the Captains. Not a patron was complaining though, as she moved about behind the bar making her job appear like an artistic performance. She went from cocktail-maker to cashier, even dart player without missing a beat. A strip of white tape was located on the floor near the end of the bar facing an electronic dartboard up against the far wall.

"Hey Maddy you're up," came from one of three men sitting at a tall table on a bar stools about ten feet away from the bar. Madeline set a drink in front of a fisherman at the bar. She rang it up on his tab, stepped from behind the bar, put her toe on the piece of tape, and tossed a dart scoring twenty points for her and her dart-throwing partner.

A pink cab pulled up out front, but no one seemed to notice. Frank got out, paid the driver and stepped into the bar. It was an average neighborhood bar with a nautical theme to it, but it didn't have the zest that the Duval street bars had. Then again those bars didn't have Madeline. She ran the show with her looks and attitude along with a louder than necessary voice that never seemed to stop. She wasn't the quiet, sensitive person Frank had met aboard his boat. While turning around to make change for someone at the pool table, she looked over and saw Frank. He was standing just inside the door letting his eyes adjust to the dim lighting. She stopped mid-sentence and smiled at him, which made every one in the bar stop what they were doing and look his way, to see what could have possibly caused her to stop talking.

"Hi Frank," she said quietly.

"Ooooo." The sound came from the men at and around the bar. Frank took a seat on the bar stool nearest the door.

"What can I get for you?" she asked, more in the sweet tone she had used during their lunch together. He hadn't noticed the two men that had came in behind him and took a seat at one of the tall tables not far from where he sat.

"A Jack and Coke would be fine." Frank answered. One of the men who had followed him in stepped up to the bar next to Frank almost touching him as he leaned toward Madeline

"Two Coronas," he said, with a thick accent that sounded Cuban. Madeline set the two beers in front of the man.

"Four dollars please," she said. The man handed her a five and went back to his table. Madeline quickly mixed a Jack and Coke for Frank.

"This one is on me," she said, looking at Frank and setting the drink in front of him.

"Hey Maddy, it's your turn," one of the men called out, holding up her darts.

"You guys go on and play without me," she answered. This brought another "Oooooo" from the crowd.

"You don't have to stop your game because of me," Frank said. "I just stopped in to have a drink."

"You could have got a drink anywhere in this town," Madeline answered smiling "But you didn't, you came here." By the time it had sunk in and Frank was prepared to answer her, she was at the other end of the bar making drinks for an older man with a young girl hanging on to his arm. The first chance she got she was standing across the bar from Frank again.

"I came in here for the free drink you promised me. Remember?" Frank said.

"Oh, I think you could have afforded to buy your own somewhere else if you would've wanted too." she said smiling. "I'm sorry I caught you off guard earlier. When I see Don he's going to hear it from me."

"Don't bother, I enjoyed talking with you today." Frank answered.

When Madeline wasn't serving customers, she was with Frank, getting to know him a little better. They talked about where they had lived before, and what type jobs each of them had at different times in their lives. Madeline told him about how she ended up in Key West and how happy she was living there. Frank mentioned that he came from Orlando and was a car salesman for the last few years. He explained how things became dull and he felt he needed a change, not wanting to go into the story of Karen. He knew it would be too hard on him to talk to someone who had never met her. Frank had a couple more drinks Madeline refused to let him pay for. Other than that the evening was laid back and casual, the way Frank liked things.

Frank left just before closing time, but not before Madeline agreed to have breakfast on his boat the next morning. The pink cab dropped him off at the Key Coast Marina that night. A late model black Chevrolet pickup had followed him from the bar. The driver with his South American-born passenger went unnoticed as they watched Frank as he boarded the *Don't Worry*. Frank slept well that night in the small berth of the little yacht.

STRANGE WIND

The sun was shining bright the next morning without a cloud in the sky. While doing a little cabin cleaning Frank heard a couple women talking up near the marina. He was coming out of the cabin with a bag of things to throw away the Harris's had left behind. One of the women turned out to be Doug making comments toward Madeline in a joking manner while she was getting a bag of groceries out of the Escort.

"My, my, my, aren't we a pretty girl today?" Doug said.

"Shut up Doug, you little smart ass," Madeline said in a way that told Frank they knew each other. She was wearing a light sundress that showed a good amount of leg. When she walked toward the pier Doug whistled after her in a way that guys do when they see an attractive woman.

"You are one hot girlfriend, girlfriend," Doug called out. Out of no where a cold chill went down Frank's spine. The thought had not crossed his mind until that second, but he was sure that, no, she couldn't be a...
But he thought he was sure of the woman he had seen at the stoplight two days ago.

"Hey handsome," Madeline said stepping aboard the boat, switching from the angry tone she was using with Doug to the sweet voice she had been using last night. She was about to go down into cabin when she saw the look on Frank's face. Her smile disappeared

"Frank, you're not thinking what I think you are, are you?" A slight whine in her voice again.

"Umm, I'm umm." is all Frank could get out.

"Fine," she said. The anger was back. "But we're still having breakfast out on the boat." She pushed past Frank and disappeared into the cabin with the grocery bag. Frank was stunned as he untied the boat and went up to the bridge. What if she wasn't a woman? He enjoyed talking to her. He could still go to the bar and talk, but he didn't know about her, or him going out on the boat or around town together. How was he supposed to find out? Maybe Don has a goofy sense of humor and was pulling a joke on him. It seems like a dumb trick to play on someone you just met, especially someone you're trying to do business with. Frank decided he would get though breakfast and ask Don about it when he went to pick up the gold shipment later. She couldn't be though... she was to feminine, wasn't she?

    A speedboat was following not too far behind off the port side. Frank was so lost in thought of whether his breakfast companion was female or just dressed that way, it could have been a battle ship and he would not have noticed it. Besides Frank had no reason to believe anyone would be spying on him.

****

    In a plush office on the ninth floor, overlooking South Beach near Miami, Eduardo Sanchez was thumping the eraser end of a pencil on his solid oak desk. He talked on the phone with his business associate, Mr. Rodriguez in South America.

    "No, no, no this will all be straightened out by the end of the week," Eduardo was saying. "We've found the fucking thief and we're on his ass right now. As a matter of fact we're following him on a run as we speak."

    "You listen to me you son of a bitch. Don't let your fuckups kill that asshole. I want to know who's behind this. If we lose another load, we lose it, but that's going to be the last of it. This guy your men are following will lead us to the man behind all of this bullshit. Don't kill a fucking fly until we know everyone involved. Then we'll kill them all! Do you understand me?" Mr. Rodriguez was not a happy man. During the last four and a half months over sixty percent of his shipment of Columbia's finest cocaine to Miami had been disappearing. He was quickly losing confidence in Eduardo, his American associate.

"Now you are sure this is the right guy?" Rodriguez asked. The last four guys they followed for days, even killing one of them by accident, ended up just being regular guys out on their boat. The poor guy they killed was fishing eight miles off the coast of Miami when his boat wouldn't start. Not knowing he was being watched he reached for a flare gun and raised it over his head. At that point he and his boat were filled with enough bullets to take out a small navy ship.

"Yeah this is the guy," Eduardo answered calmly.

"All right then, lets wrap this job up so we can get back to business," Rodriguez said and hung up the phone.

****

Frank dropped anchor about ten miles out from Key Coast Marina and sat down at the table on the deck of the *Don't Worry* and waited, not wanting to go down into the cabin.

"Frank, could you come down here for a minute please?" Madeline called from the cabin. Frank hesitated, but made his way though the hatch.

"Could you put this stuff here out on the table please?" Madeline asked in her sweet tone of voice again before Frank was all the way down the ladder.

"Yeah, sure," Frank answered just as his head cleared the hatch, and then he froze. Standing in front of him stood Madeline with a spatula in her hand tending to a couple of eggs frying in a skillet on the stove like Frank wasn't even there. All of her clothes were neatly folded and lying on the sofa toward the bow. Frank could see her from head to toe from her left side. She was completely naked. Madeline turned toward him with the spatula still in her hand.

"Are you satisfied?" she said, slightly spreading her arms. "Can we please put this behind us?" He didn't mean to but he couldn't help from looking her up and down, twice. Not only was she a woman, she was beautiful, not a flaw on her body, but she was big. Frank then hung his head in shame.

"I'm so sorry, I never should have doubted it, please forgive me." She pressed her body to his and with the hand that was not holding the utensil she lifted his head and kissed him on the cheek.

"It's okay," she said almost whispering. "Unfortunately I get that a lot since I moved down here. Now take this stuff upstairs so I can get my clothes back on." She handed him two plates stacked with napkins, forks and a couple other breakfast related items. Frank took the items up the ladder and placed everything on the table and sat down. Madeline came out on the deck still in the nude for just a second to put a platter of eggs and hash browns on the table. Then she went back down the companionway into the cabin to get dressed.

****

Standing on the deck of the speedboat not far away, Anthony Lopez watched the action on the *Don't Worry* though his binoculars. He noticed the larger person wasn't wearing any clothes, but was too far away to tell much else. He lowered the binoculars and could see how it was all coming together now.

"I've got this whole thing all figured out," he said to Paul his partner, and also younger brother. Paul was seated at the helm of their low-slung boat downing the last of his beer.

"Let's head on in so we can report back to Uncle Eduardo and let him know what we've found out," Anthony said. He put away the binoculars and fell into the seat next to his brother. Paul threw the empty bottle into the ocean, then started the engine and spun the boat around in the direction of Key West.

****

Madeline came back on deck, fully dressed this time, and with two glasses of orange juice. Frank started to apologize, but she stopped him by pushing her finger to his lips.

"I said we would put it behind us. Now let's just forget the whole thing even happened," Madeline said, and that was the last of it. Frank felt good about the whole incident. Now there was no doubt about the situation, and a beautiful naked woman had kissed him. That part he wouldn't forget. He wondered if he should give her what was left of Wally's forty dollars, since she was the first nude woman he had seen. He decided that would not be a good idea.

Once again they had a nice time together and made plans to go to the State Park for a swim and a little sightseeing in Madeline's car the next morning. She wouldn't have to be at work until later that day for the Thursday night football crowd. Frank docked the boat back at the usual slip and walked Madeline up to her car.

"I'll see you tomorrow," he said, as she got into the little Ford.

"Okay, I'll see you then," she said and drove away. Other than the kiss on the check in the cabin, and a gentle touch here and there, they had little contact.

CHAPTER 13

    Frank got on his bike. As he headed out of the marina parking lot, he noticed a black Chevrolet pickup truck pull away from the curb. It drove past him in a big hurry. He watched it go down Front Street to the corner of Duval Street, where it stop and waited until Frank peddled by. The driver took off and past him again, then turned right on Green Street. Frank thought it seemed a little odd the way the dark complexioned man was driving, and by the way he had stared at him as he drove, but in Key West odd was to be expected. Frank parked his bike on the sidewalk and walked into Don's pawnshop. Don was arranging some watches in a glass case from behind the counter.
    "Hey, there you are, you're a little early but that's okay. I have everything ready to go for you," he said. Don noticed a funny little smile on Frank's face. "Is every thing alright?"
    "Yeah everything's fine. By the way, I met Madeline," Frank answered.
    "You did, well, that's great. She's a real nice girl don't you think?" Don asked not knowing why Frank was grinning. "What's the matter, you said you were all by yourself didn't you? She's great company. I go to Captain

Crabbies sometimes just to talk to her. Since she moved into the apartment above my garage several years ago, my wife and I think of her as family." Frank had never thought to ask her where she lived. They had met either at the bar or the *Don't Worry*.

"Frank, let me give you one piece of advice about dealing with that woman," Don said, looking very serious. "If you two don't agree on something, it would be best if you let her have her way. I saw her throw a guy out of the bar one night right into the street, and he never touched the sidewalk." Frank looked at him like he was kidding. She had the size for it, but she was just too sweet he thought.

"Well, if that's true I'm sure he deserved it. He must have grabbed her breast or something like that," Frank said, forcing a little laugh.

"Nope, it was nothing like that," Don said, shaking his head. "She tossed him out because he said the Redskins were gonna beat the crap out of the Dolphins. You a Dolphin fan Frank?" Strange question, Frank thought.

"They're okay I guess, but I'm more of a Buccaneers fan myself." Frank said.

"You might want to rethink that if you're going to keep seeing Madeline," Don said, with a chuckle.

Across the street from the pawnshop Anthony and Paul were sitting in their Chevy truck. Anthony was on a cell phone with his Uncle Eduardo in Miami.

"Yeah, yeah that's right, it's a three man operation," Anthony was saying with an arrogant cockiness to his voice. "We already knew who the guy was intercepting the shipments. Now we know who the ringleader is. He's running the operation out of a pawnshop down here. We found out today they've got some drag queen that is distributing the goods for them."

Just then Frank came out of the shop with the suitcase full of gold-plated crap not noticing the truck down the street. He strapped the suitcase to the bike and headed back to Key Coast. After the goods and bike were loaded on the boat he untied the *Don't Worry* and began the cruise to Bimini. Frank looked back as Key West was slipping out of sight. A lot of his idle time was still filled with memories of Karen. He missed her dearly, but somehow he thought she would approve of him spending time with Madeline, because Madeline was the total opposite of Karen. It wasn't like he was trying to replace her. Karen was small and petite and Madeline, well Madeline was not. Karen was friendly and kind to everyone and Madeline, although sweet to him he'd seen, and heard stories about her rougher side. Karen was full of confidence and didn't care what anyone thought of her, but Madeline was self-conscience of her size and appearance. Frank's mind was so occupied with thoughts of how he felt about Madeline that he ended up in Bimini almost without knowing how he got there.

    Frank walked into Dorrey's shop and set the suitcase on the counter.

    "Hey how are you? It's Frank right?" Dorrey said. "Please excuse me one moment." He picked up the phone and quickly dialed a number. He spoke in a low tone, something in Spanish, then hung up. Dorrey came around the counter and began the same process as before. He looked over the trinkets closely, then gave Frank back the empty suitcase and a envelope full of cash.

    Frank took his bike out on the sidewalk, strapped the empty suitcase on the rack behind the seat and took off down the road. He peddled along the narrow street headed back to the marina where the *Don't Worry* waited. Two men dressed in black pants, and white tank tops jumped out from behind a dumpster. They knocked Frank off the bicycle and jumped on top of him. He had no idea what was going on.

After a quick scuffle with the men, where Frank got in a few good licks of his own, they were gone. Frank felt blood trickling down his cheek from a cut above his left eye. He pressed his hand against the cut and stood up. He felt a slight pain in his right leg, but figured it was nothing that he couldn't walk off. He reached for the envelope of cash that was last seen in his shirt pocket. It was no longer there. He could see his bike laying half on the sidewalk and half on the street. Surprised that they hadn't taken the bike he limped over to it. Lying on the ground beside it was the envelope still sealed. Frank picked it up and put it back in his pocket and got on the bike. He was a bit wobbly at first, but was able to make it back to the waterfront.

Not until he arrived at the boat did he realize that the suitcase was missing. He put his bike away and began untying the *Don't Worry* when a speedboat zipped past, heading northwest towards Miami. Frank wondered if he should have gone to the marina office and tried to contact the Bimini police department to report the attack. Since he wasn't hurt too bad, and didn't really get a good look at the attackers, he decided against it. They only got away with an old used suitcase anyway. He figured he probably did the right thing. They might have turned it around somehow and thrown him in jail. He thought he would just be more careful next time.

Frank went down into the cabin and washed the blood off his face before climbing up to the helm and heading for his homeport. After a couple hours of cruising along all of a sudden the *Don't Worry* cut out, then picked up speed and cut out again. Frank thought he could see the lights of Key West just peeking over the horizon. The engine took off again for a few hundred yards and cut out. Frank pulled back on the throttle lever until he was at an idle, then eased back into it. The boat moved up on a plane as he continued to throttle up. Once again it started to spit and sputter. Frank throttled down until it smoothed out to a slow but steady pace. He figured it was just a clogged fuel filter or water in the gas and that he shouldn't have to radio for help.

Frank slowly pulled the *Don't Worry* up into its slip at Key Coast about an hour or so later. He let out a sigh of relief that he had made it back. Between getting beat up, loosing Don's suitcase, and now the mechanical problems with the boat, Frank considered himself lucky to be back in Key West in one piece.

CHAPTER 14

The next morning, while waiting for Madeline to arrive, Frank went up to the office of the marina. Doug was behind the counter talking on the phone, apparently a personal phone call.

"Phone book?" Frank spoke quietly so not to interrupt anything. Doug rolled his eyes at Frank and handed him a phone book from underneath the counter. Frank laid the book open on the counter and thumbed through the yellow pages until he located the listings under boat repair. He went though the company names but could not find the Magic Wizard listing he was looking for. He remembered seeing the name on the truck not long after his arrival in Key West. Doug was just hanging up the phone when Frank looked over the counter at the young man.

"Do you know the number to the Magic Wizard?" Frank asked Doug who was lazily chewing gum.

"No, but I just got off the phone with the tooth fairy."

You want me to call her back for you?" Doug laughed. Now Frank rolled his eyes.

"It a boat mechanic called The Magic Wizard Boat Repair. I saw their truck here the other day."

"Never heard of them, are you having trouble with your boat?" Doug asked. He was a homosexual smart-ass but Frank didn't care, actually he thought it was kind of funny.

"Yeah it started cutting out on me yesterday and I need to find someone to take a look at it," Frank answered.

"Well, we have always used Lower Keys Mobile Marine Service," Doug said. "You want me to call them for you?"

"Yes, if you would please that would be great." Frank answered. Doug dialed the number from memory then handed the phone to Frank. He explained what had happened with his boat and made arrangements for him to come out later that day. The mechanic asked Frank to leave the ignition key with Doug so he could check everything out and find the problem. Frank handed the receiver back to Doug who had heard the conversation and picked up the boat key off the counter. Before returning the receiver to its cradle, Doug held it to his ear as Frank was turning to leave

"Hello, Magic Wizard?" Doug was saying into the dead phone. "Yes, I have the secret key, come quickly." He held the boat key high over his head laughing. Frank laughed too. Gay or not that was damn funny he thought.

****

In Eduardo's office in South Beach his two nephews stood in front of his desk with a black suitcase a little bigger than a briefcase sitting on the desk.

"What the fuck is this?" Eduardo said angrily gesturing towards the suitcase.

"That's yesterday's shipment of coke. We got it back for you." Paul told his uncle.

"Forty kilos of cocaine is in that suitcase?" Eduardo said with sarcasm in his voice. He pushed the case gently with one finger; it rocked back and forth before tipped over on the desk.

"Did it ever occur to you two knuckleheads that this thing feels empty?" pulling at his collar, trying not to lose his cool.

"We grabbed it right after the son of a bitch picked it up ther..." Eduardo raised his hand stopped Anthony mid sentence.

"Open it." Eduardo said looking directly at Anthony.

"What?"

"Open the damn case," Eduardo said leaning forward across the desk. Anthony pulled the two levers on each side and lifted the top. The three men looked inside. It was empty. Paul started pacing the floor running his fingers though his thick black hair.

"Unbelievable! Un-fucking-believable!" He was talking to himself looking up at the ceiling. Eduardo reached into the case, and in between his thick finger and fat thumb, he pulled out what appeared to be a tiny gold colored charm molded into the shape of a tiny little duck.

"Wait a minute, wait just one minute," Eduardo said raising the cheap little trinket up to the light. "This wasn't a lost cause after all. Do you know what this means?" Paul stopped pacing and hurried over to the desk next to his brother to see what kind of clue the tiny charm may hold. Maybe their trip to Bimini was not in vain after all and the little duck would be the missing key to the location of the cocaine.

"Do you know why there is a golden duck in this suitcase?" Eduardo said, in a low tone. The two younger men shook their heads and leaned in closer to get a better look at the tiny piece of gold.

"This duck is in this suitcase as a reminder," Eduardo whispered. "It's here to remind me that you two idiots are as worthless as a pimple on a duck's ass!" Eduardo got louder and louder with each word until he was screaming and his face was turning red. He threw the golden duck across the room. As soon as he stopped screaming he fought to regain control.

"Look," he said, rubbing his hand over his face. "Now I know we are on the right track. What we're dealing with here are real professionals, but now it's time we send them a little message. A message that we know who they are, and that this shit is gonna come to a stop. Do you understand what I'm saying?"

Just then the phone on the desk began to ring.

"Yeah," Eduardo said, as he picked up the receiver.

"Has our little problem been taken care of yet?" Mr. Rodriguez's voice came hauntingly though the line.

"As a matter of fact I've got the boys here right now. We were just discussing the situation," Eduardo answered.

"I see," Mr. Rodriguez said. "So, what have you and the boy's found out so far?"

"It's a three man ring. They're operating out of Key West," Eduardo said. He flipped open a cedar lined box on his desk and took out a fine hand-rolled Cuban cigar.

"Key fucking West, are you out of your mind? Why would they smuggle the shit into Key West. It goes into Miami and then moves north. Why the hell would they take it to Key West?" Rodriguez was losing his cool. His only connection in the United States and he doesn't even know the normal flow of coke in his own country. Even the Feds know it comes in through Miami and then is smuggled north up I-95. Eduardo didn't flinch one bit as he dragged a wooden match along the underside of his oak desk and lit his cigar.

"They operate out of Key West," he said calmly. "Because they know we wouldn't look for them in Key West. North of Miami is where they think we would look. These guys are pros. There not fucking around. If they didn't know what the hell they were doing they would be wearing concrete boots at the bottom of the ocean by now." Eduardo puffed on the stogie. Rodriguez was quiet. How dumb could he be? Of course they were pros if they were able to steal from him and his men.

"I see, then do whatever you have to do. Let's wrap this up as soon as we can. It's costing us a lot of dough." Click, the line was dead.

CHAPTER 15

    Madeline picked Frank up at his boat the next morning and drove to Fort Zachary Taylor State Park near the southern end of Key West. They toured the fort and even held hands part of the time. Around noon they went for a swim in the cool Atlantic Ocean and sat on the beach. They had cheese and crackers and a bottle of white wine that Madeline brought along.
After the light snack they left the car at the park and walked up Truman Avenue looking in several of the shops in that area of Key West. Not really shopping but just spending time together. Before they knew it the sun was beginning to sink into the western sky and Madeline had to be at work. They headed back to the car and Frank drove the short distance to Key Coast Marina. When they reached the marina parking lot, and got out of the car, Frank touched Madeline on the arm to turn her toward him. She was looking him in the eyes and lifted her hand

to his shoulder.

"I had a real nice time today," Frank said softly.

"I did too," Madeline said, as she tilted her head and closed her eyes, Frank leaned forward.

"Maddy, yo, Maddy," someone shouted. It startled them both as they looked across the parking lot of the marina.

"Hey, are you on your way to the Captain's?" A man in a faded out T-shirt and sand colored camouflaged shorts called out. They hung below his knees with frayed strings hanging even lower because they used to be pants at one time. He was walking their direction.

"That's Dan, a guy I know from the bar," she said to Frank while giving a wave Dan's way. She only knew him as the guy that chased shots of vodka with Coors Light.

In a much louder voice called out in Dan's direction. "Yeah Dan, I'm heading that way in just a minute."

"Hey that's great!" he called out. "Could I catch a ride with you? I want to go up there and watch the football game tonight." Dan worked at the Ocean Foam Car Wash, but was just waiting for his big break into the hard rock scene as a lead guitarist. Dan started to walk a little faster as if trying not to keep her waiting. Frank and Madeline were trying so hard not to start laughing; they couldn't have kissed for nothing at this point. Dan had reached the car and was already climbing into the passenger side even though Madeline hadn't exactly said "yes" to his request.

"Are you going to come up to Captain Crabbies and watch the game with us?" Madeline said, still standing face to face with Frank. Before Frank had a chance to answer, Dan leaned over toward the driver's window.

"It's gonna be a kick ass game man. Tennessee and Philadelphia, you should come dude." They could no longer hold back the laugher.

"No, no, I think I'll watch it here on the boat and take it

easy tonight." Frank said to Madeline.

"Okay man, have a good one dude," came from inside the car. Madeline got in the car still smiling at Frank.

"Sorry," she whispered. Frank stood and watched until her taillights were out of sight, then made his way back to his boat.

Frank sat out on the deck with a cold beer, watching the game on a small portable TV. It was a beautiful night, the stars were out, and a gentle wind was blowing in from the west. Nice and peaceful the way Frank liked it.

Captain Crabbies was packed, smoky, and loud, with football fans everywhere. The waitresses were serving drinks as fast as Madeline could get them up on the bar. Dan, trying to repay the favor of the ride, would run five-gallon buckets of ice from the ice maker in the back up to the bar for Madeline when he wasn't busy hollering for the Eagles on one of the six TVs around the bar room. The game took on a whole new meaning to Dan since he had made a twenty-dollar bet on the game with Bubba, another of the Captain Crabbies regulars. Bubba was at the Captains almost every evening. He would usually have his boss drop him off after work. After mowing grass all day he would work up quite a thirst for a couple of beers. The game was down to three and a half minutes left in the fourth quarter, and the Eagles were up by seventeen. Dan was feeling pretty good when the Titans fumbled and Philadelphia recovered. Bubba threw up his hands and let out a few choice words directed toward one of the televisions. He downed the last of his beer and stomped toward the door, throwing a crumpled twenty on the bar.

Once the game ended the bar began to clear out a little. Some of the waitresses began wiping off tables and gathering up the empty beer bottles and glasses left behind. Dan ordered one more beer and gave Madeline a five-dollar tip out of his newfound wealth. Just as she picked up the tip something exploded out front. Orange flames were reflecting on the glass of the large window facing the street. Madeline and some of the others picked themselves up from the floor; others were running out the door to see what had happened. Madeline quickly dialed 911 and was told to stay on the line, as one of the waitresses came back in the door.

"Maddy, it's your car!" she said.

"What! Here take the phone." Madeline handed the waitress the phone over the bar and ran for the door. When she got outside she could see the outline of her little car in the glowing flames. Dan came up behind her and put his hand on her shoulder.

"Maddy, I'm so sorry, I don't know what to say," he said.

"It's not your fault," Madeline said, pressing a napkin to her eyes.

"Someone said they saw Bubba hanging around your car just before it blew up," Dan said. "Maybe he saw me ride up here with you and was trying to get even with me for the twenty bucks he lost. He wasn't very happy when he left."

Police reports were taken and Bubba was the lead suspect. Madeline finished her work at the bar and called a cab to take her home.

CHAPTER 16

Frank started a pot of coffee and went to get the morning paper from the paper box in front of the marina's office as the sun crept higher and higher into the sky. **CAR FIRE AT LOCAL NIGHTSPOT** was splashed across the front page. He tucked the paper under his arm and went back to his boat. He tossed it on the deck table and went down into the cabin for a cup of coffee. Once back on deck he opened the paper to the sports section to see who won the game last night. He had fallen asleep before it ended. Not until he folded the paper and laid it down on the table did he see the bright colors of ink that could only represent a fire. He looked out over the ocean and took a sip of his coffee, before it hit him that he had heard a loud boom last night that had caused him to stir. Frank unfolded the paper and laid it out on the table so he could read the story without holding it. The large picture on the front page was of a ball of fire. A smaller picture was at the lower left-hand corner. In the smaller picture was Madeline with her hands to her mouth, standing on the sidewalk in front of Captain Crabbies, crying. Frank slowly sat down his coffee.

"Oh my god, Madeline!" He spoke aloud, although no

one was around to hear him. Frank was in shock; he didn't know what to do. He had never asked her for her phone number or where she lived. "What kind of boyfriend would not know his girlfriends phone number?" he thought.

"Oh my god," he said again, but this time for thinking boyfriend, girlfriend, instead of just friends. "Oh my god, oh my god, oh my god." He knew she was okay physically because of the picture, but he felt he had to see her.

Frank hurried down into the cabin and grabbed his wallet then took off up front street to flag down a cab.

"Take me to Captain Crabbies," Frank said, as he climbed into the back seat of the pink car.

"Kind of early for a drink, ain't it buddy?" the driver said, just trying to make conversation.

"I'm looking for my girlfr..., I mean, a friend of mine." Frank answered, although a straight shot of whiskey didn't sound like a bad idea to calm the nerves a little. The cab pulled over to the curb in front of the bar where Madeline worked. Frank could see the scorched pavement and the burned grass between the road and the sidewalk.

"Wait here for a minute, I'll be right back," Frank said to the cab driver and ran into the bar. Things were just barely stirring this early in the morning at the Captain's, only a bartender and two older gentlemen were at the bar.

"Can you tell me where I might find Madeline?" Frank asked the bartender.

"Who?" The bartender answered.

"Madeline, the lady who was tending bar here last night," Frank said.

"Oh, you must mean Maddy," the bartender looked at Frank suspiciously. "You wouldn't be the asshole that set her car on fire last night would you?" The thought of him doing anything to hurt Madeline hit Frank like a ton of bricks.

"What! Hell no. I'm a friend of hers. I want to make sure she's alright," Frank said.

"She's fine, don't you worry about it pal," the bartender said, in a not so friendly tone. Frank let out a sigh, his shoulders slumped, he hung his head.

"Listen pal," the bartender spoke again but in a more sympathetic voice. "Even if I wanted to tell you where she was I couldn't, because I don't know where she lives myself. Sorry man." Frank thanked him and went back out to the cab.

"She's not here. Do you know where Don Golden Pawn is?" Frank asked the driver.

"Sure pal, I know where it's at," the driver answered and pulled back out into traffic. It was eight fifteen when they stopped in front of the pawnshop. Don didn't open until nine.

"Shit!" Frank said. "How much do I owe you? I guess I'll get out here." He was reaching for his wallet.

"Are you looking for the lady whose car blew up last night?" the driver asked. Frank could only stare at the man momentarily before he could answer.

"Yes, I am. Do you know where I might find her?" he finally was able to say.

"I don't know if I should tell you this or not, but I'm the guy that drove her home last night. I could take you to where I dropped her off." Reaching toward Frank he rubbed his thumb and two of his fingers together. Frank quickly gave the man two twenty-dollar bills and jumped back into the cab. The driver put the cab in drive and hit the gas. Soon they were out of the business section of town; bars and shell shops gave way to houses and apartment buildings. They turned down a narrow shell covered road and stopped in front of a house you could barely see because of the thick foliage growing around it.

"This is where she got out, that's all I know," the driver said and Frank handed him another twenty and waved off the change.
"By the way," Frank leaned down to talk into the driver's window, "How was she last night?"
"She'd been crying a little, but seemed okay I guess." The driver nodded his head in thanks for the tip and drove away.
Frank remembered Don saying she lived above the garage so he headed around the side of the house. Pushing hibiscus limbs out of his way as he walked, he came across a one-car garage with a narrow flight of wooden steps going up the far side. Frank looked around the small yard then began up the steps. He wondered what Madeline would do when she saw him. Would she think he was stalking her, or feel he was getting too attached to be coming to her house uninvited? Or maybe she didn't want him to know where she lived. Frank was now at the top of the stairs, facing the door. Maybe he should leave? No he couldn't, whether it upset her or not, he had to know she was okay. Frank knocked.
"Who is it?" Madeline said from behind the door in a guarded voice.
"It's me, Frank." He heard a deadbolt unlock and the door quickly opened. Madeline was out on the little balcony and in Frank's arms before he knew what had happened.
"Are you alright?" he asked.
"Yes, I'm fine. I'm just a little shaken," Madeline said. Frank could tell she'd been crying. He knew exactly how it felt to loose something important. Of course loosing a wife is on a different level than a car, but he still knew how she must feel. Frank put the idea of her being upset with him out of his mind.
They walked into the small apartment. It was decorated

the way only a woman could decorate. Small pillows were perfectly placed on the couch like it wasn't made to sit on. There were doilies on the arms of an upholstered chair. Porcelain figurines sitting on and around a television set. The small wooden dining room table was covered with a white lace tablecloth. If Frank had seen this earlier, Madeline wouldn't have had to take her clothes off on the boat.

"I don't know what I'm going to do without my car." Madeline said, as she sat down on the edge of one of the dining room chairs. Frank didn't think much about the little car. He was used to luxury cars and convertibles, but he knew that the car had meant a lot to Madeline.

"I can't afford to replace it. Taxi fees are going to be hard enough." Madeline was thinking out loud. Frank was doing some thinking of his own.

"Do you have a phone I could use?" he asked.

"What, oh, I'm sorry, sure there's one in the bedroom. Can I get you a cup of coffee or something?"

"Coffee would be fine," Frank said.

Frank sat on the edge of the bed and pulled out a business card from his wallet. He dialed the number.

"Crystal River Marina, Sam speaking. Can I help you?" a loud voice said.

"Yes is Wally around?" Frank asked.

"Hang on a minute," Frank waited.

"This is Wally," a man said.

"Wally this is Frank, I met you last week, I bought the Harris's yacht remember?"

"The *Don't Worry,* yeah I remember, you were going to Key West right, is she okay?" Wally said.

"Is who okay?" Frank asked.

"The boat, is she alright?" Wally answered.

"Oh, yeah she's fine but I was calling about the Toyota. Is it still there?" Frank heard the sound of tobacco juice

hitting the concrete floor of the shop.
"Unless it set out on its own last night it's right where you left it. Hey, have you seen any of them nude girls running around down there yet?" Wally said, lowering his voice.
"Well, actually I have seen one. How would you like to come down here and check it out for yourself this weekend?"
"You say you've seen one huh?" Wally said, like he thought Frank was withholding important information from him. Surely he'd seen more than one. Frank was starting to think this was going to be harder than he thought.
"Wally, I need my car down here and if you could drive it down here tonight when you get off work, you could stay the weekend and I'll pay for everything." Frank waited for an answer.
"Wally?"
"Yeah."
"Did you hear me?"
"Yeah."
"Well, what do you think?" Frank said.
"You say you saw at least one huh?" Wally was thinking over the proposition.
"Yeah, I've seen at least one. She was on my boat." Frank's brain was trying to come up with an alternative plan to help out Madeline.
"Jumped right on your boat I bet," Wally said.
"It was something like that," Frank answered.
"Okay I'll be there around nine o'clock," Wally blurted out.
"I'm sorry, what was that?" Frank thought his ears had deceived him.
"Yeah, maybe you're right Frank, fuck the boss. I'll leave a couple hours early. I can be there around seven.

What's the name of the marina you're moored at?"

"Did I say fuck the boss?" Frank thought, "I didn't say fuck the boss."

"I'm docked at Key Coast Marina. I'll keep an eye out for you," he said.

"Hey Frank, did you see her before seven o'clock, or after seven?" Wally asked.

"Who, the *Don't Worry?*

"No, the naked girl that jumped on your boat." Boy this guy has got a one-track mind Frank thought.

"Umm, let's see. It was before seven." Frank said, not really lying but it wasn't exactly the truth either.

"Oh it was?" Wally said, as if he thought Frank wasn't being honest again.

"Alright then I'll see you tonight." Frank hung up the phone and believed he would probably never see Wally or his little car again.

Frank went back into the only other room, except for the tiny bathroom. Madeline was sitting at the dining table with two cups of coffee.

"I made a long distance call on your phone. I'll pay for it when you get the bill," he said. Madeline didn't respond.

"Do you have to work tonight?" Frank asked, just trying to start a conversation and get Madeline's mind off the car situation.

"Yes, I have to be there at five o'clock," she answered.

Frank slowly got Madeline to start talking and looking ahead, instead of at what had already happened. By lunchtime, Madeline was feeling much better thanks to Frank for being there with her. Frank hadn't mentioned the car and Wally, because he didn't want to let her down in case they never showed up. He would have put money against it if he had to choose. Madeline was going to fix some soup and a couple of sandwiches for lunch, but

Frank suggested they go out instead. Thinking it might help to make her feel better. They went to a restaurant within walking distance of her apartment and far from the tourist-type establishments of the Old Town area. They had cheeseburgers, fries and root beers and talked about everything from Dan's football bet to why Frank put his ketchup on his plate and dipped his fries in it and Madeline poured it all over the top of her fries. Frank even had Madeline laughing about her little bar-b-qued car before they returned to her apartment.

"Would you like to come up for a little while?" Madeline said, as they stood at the bottom of the wooden stairs. She said it in a way that made Frank think there was an insinuation of sex in the comment.

"No, I think I better go," not wanting to take advantage of the lovely Madeline when she was in such a vulnerable state.

"That would probably be best I guess," she said, seeing his point and thankful for his compassion.

"I'll come by and see you tonight at the Captain's," he said, looking around to see if Dan was going to pop up and ruin the moment again. Madeline lowered her eyes as Frank stepped forward. He held out his right hand palm up, and Madeline laid her left hand in it. He touched her cheek with his other hand moving his thumb below her eye as if to wipe away a tear, she smiled, she liked Frank and….

"Frank, is that you Frank? hey Frank."

"You've got to be kidding me," Frank thought. He could not believe he was not going to get to kiss her again. He turned around and saw Don, coming down the back steps of his house.

"Frank. Boy am I glad I caught you," Don said, walking across the lawn.

"Wow, what luck, I was just about to leave," Frank

Said, looking at Madeline who was doing her best not to crack up laughing.

"What's so funny?" Don asked.

"Nothing Don, nothing at all. What do you need to talk to me about?" Frank said giving Madeline a playful push on her shoulder.

"I got a call from Dorrey this morning. Can you make a run in the morning for me?" Frank looked toward Don, then back at Madeline.

"Would you like to take a cruise to Bimini with me tomorrow morning?" he asked. She shrugged her large beautiful shoulders.

"Sure, why not? That sounds like fun," Madeline answered with a smile.

"Okay Don. I'll make a run tomorrow, no problem," Frank said in his direction, then turned back to Madeline.

"Well I guess I'll see you tonight," he said, and kissed her on the cheek.

"I'll be looking for you," she said putting her hand over the cheek he had kissed.

****

In a hotel room near Smathers Beach Anthony and Paul were in disbelief as they stared at the newspaper.

"A fucking lawn maintenance guy, they think a fucking lawn maintenance guy blew up that thieving, drug smugglers shitty car!" Anthony was screaming. "We send them the message that we're on to them and the cops blame some asshole grass cutter. Look at this damn picture!" He showed the paper to Paul, who had already seen it, but looked at it again anyway.

"That damn drag queen standing there like he's some kind of innocent victim, crying like a little girl. Tonight they are going down Paul, no one makes a fool out of us two times in a row and gets away with it."

"Right!" Paul said, getting fired up. "Nobody makes a fool out of us, but me and you." Just then the phone rang. Anthony picked it up Eduardo was furious.

"What the fuck are you two clowns doing down there? Are you the ones that blew up that lady's car?"

Anthony held the receiver away from his head as his uncle continued.

"Congratulations you made the news all the way to Miami you assholes." Eduardo dumped six of his high blood pressure pills out of the bottle that informed him to only take two. He threw them into the back of his throat and washed them down with a shot of vodka sitting on his desk for this purpose.

"I knew as soon as I saw it that it was you fucking guys."

"He's the guy that distributes the coke. We were sending him a message not to fuck with us," Anthony said with a certain amount of forcefulness.

"He! You stupid moron that was a woman's car, I saw her crying on the ten o'clock news." Anywhere else it was pretty clear that Madeline was a woman, but in Key West nothing was a sure thing.

"He's in drag boss. It's not a woman, its a man dressed up like a woman, so you won't suspect him and he can conceal more cocaine in women's clothing and get away with it than he can dressed as a man. Down here all men wear is shorts and a T-shirt or they stick out like a sore thumb. Women can get by wearing anything they want and it doesn't look suspicious," Anthony said it as if he was trying to show his uncle how smart he was.

"So you and Paul, you guys running around down there in short pants?" Eduardo asked.

"Hell no, we ain't no sissies," Anthony said defensively. Eduardo was starting to sweat through his silk suit even though the air conditioner was on high in the big office with its high priced furnishings.

"Look, we know for a fact they're intercepting the shipment with a boat, right?"

"Yeah boss," Anthony answered.

"Then why the fuck did you blow up a car?" Eduardo was at the top of his lungs and standing up now.

"Oh yeah, yeah boss I see where you're coming from, I see," Anthony said. Something about if you weren't my sister's kids and then a slamming of the receiver came though the phone.

"Paul, I got an idea. Come here."

Chapter 17

Back at Key Coast Frank settled the bill with Doug for the repairs to his boat.
"Are you going to take it out for a test run?" Doug asked. Frank hadn't thought about it, but it made sense before heading over to the Bahamas again.
"Yeah, I guess that would be the smart thing to do," Frank said, as he was about to walk out the door.
"You care if I come along?" Doug asked. Frank was caught off guard by the question. He didn't know how to answer. There was no reason to not let him come along but why did he want too?
"I was a guy before I was gay. I like sports, cars and boats just like any other guy." Doug said, seeing Frank's confusion.
"Yeah, sure, why not, come on," Frank said. Doug let out a little scream and came bouncing around the counter. Frank immediately wondered what had he just done. Doug

hung a little sign on the door in the shape of a clock that read "be back at." Doug moved the little red plastic hands of the clock to read thirty minutes in the future. Frank and Doug walked down the dock toward the *Don't Worry* while a pelican sat perched on a post that was sticking up out of the water nearby. After untying the boat they both climbed up the ladder to the bridge. Doug stood with his hands on top of the windshield as Frank maneuvered the *Don't Worry* out of the slip and into the open ocean. Soon they were speeding along the coastline at a pretty good speed. The engines were performing as they should and Doug seemed to be enjoying the wind and sun. Frank throttled down to a slower speed.

"You get out here on the water very often?" Frank asked.

"Nope, actually this is my first time," Doug said still looking straight ahead.

"Are you kidding me? You work at a marina and you've never been out on a boat?" Frank said quite surprised. Doug just shook his head. Frank looked over the dashboard; everything seemed to be in order.

"You want to steer?" Frank asked

"What! Are you serious?" Doug said he had never had a straight man do anything nice for him, except for maybe his family and sometime they weren't very friendly to him either. He was already thrilled just by the fact that he was even out on the boat.

"Hell yeah, that would be great!" Doug said. Frank showed him the way to work the throttle and told him to make smooth movements with the steering wheel and stepped aside to let Doug take over. Captain Doug did exactly what Frank told him to do as they took the *Don't Worry* on up the coast, and turned around to come back. As they got closer to the marina Frank took over at the helm, and put her back in the slip. Doug jumped off and tied the boat to the dock.

"Thanks Frank. That was the most fun I've had in a long time. I'm going to see if I can't get you a discount on your slip rental when I see my dad again." He skipped like a little girl back to the marina office. Frank shook his head, smiled, and then went down into the cabin to get ready to go out.

Anthony and Paul were in their boat not far away watching as the two docked the *Don't Worry*.

"This is one sick fucking bunch were dealing with here." Anthony said, watching Doug return to the marina office.

"I can't believe we're getting ripped off by a bunch of faggots, Paul said pushing his sunglasses up on his forehead. Anthony lowered the binoculars and motioned for Paul to start up their boat and head back to the hotel.

CHAPTER 18

A few hours after Frank and Doug's little joy ride, the sun was slipping into the ocean. A vehicle pulled into the Key Coast Marina. Anthony and Paul watched from their truck, parked on the other side of the small inlet, waiting to see when they could get aboard Frank's boat without being seen. A man got out of the car and took a canvas bag from the back seat. The tall figure walked through the darkness toward the docks. Quietly, he made his way among the docked vessels until he came to the *Don't Worry*. Frank came out of the cabin just as the man was about to step aboard the yacht. Startled, he stumbled backwards against the boat's cabin until his eyes focused.

"Wally? Wally, you son of a gun you made it!" Frank exclaimed. "How did the Toyota run?"

"Yep, I made it, but I did have a tire blow out just below Marathon." Wally put his fist up like he was holding the steering wheel and shook his hands around in a violent motion to show how the car reacted to the flat tire as he spit tobacco juice on the dock. "Luckily the spare was in good shape and I got her changed. Have there been any nudies running around yet?" Wally looked along the shoreline surrounding the inlet.

"No, I hadn't seen any out yet, but I was just about to go to Captain Crabbies over on Simonton Street if you want to come along?" Frank said expecting Wally to say "yes."

"No thanks, I think I'll go get me a hotel room and check out Duval Street." Wally tilted his head forward. "That's where the action is you know," he said, letting Frank know he was a man about town.

"I could drop you off anywhere you want me to," Frank said. Wally handed him the Toyota keys and spit more dark juice that splattered on the dock next to Frank's boat.

"That's alright, I'd rather walk, you know, kind of get a feel for the town if you know what I mean," Wally said.

"Sure, whatever you want to do is fine with me," Frank said, as he took out his wallet. "I sure do want to thank you for bringing the car down. How does two hundred dollars sound?"

"That sounds about right. I'll get me a room, go have some drinks, and watch for the girls. I'll stop by your boat tomorrow some time," Wally said. He put the money in his pocket, picked up his duffel bag and took off across the parking lot. Frank closed the hatch on the cabin and left for Captain Crabbies in the little car.

Not long after Frank and the Toyota pulled away from the marina, a black Chevy pickup pulled in. Two men got out and made their way along the docks with what looked like a bowling bag with them. Once they were near Frank's yacht they squatted down in the darkness. Paul opened up the bag and set the timing device inside it. Anthony spotted dark splotches on the dock right next to where they were kneeling.

"Hurry up damn it, let's get the hell out of here." Anthony said, staring at the splotches.

"I've almost got it, hang on," Paul said. At that moment two of the biggest hands he ever seen on a person wearing a yellow sequined evening gown grabbed him by the belt and back of his neck and threw him off the dock along with the bowling bag. When Anthony saw the sparkling Amazon, he quickly turned to make a run for the truck. A smaller figure was standing between him and the shoreline swinging a boat anchor over his head attached to a rope. With a lunge and a grunt the anchor came down across Anthony's back right between his shoulder blades causing him to tumble into the dark waters below, not far from where his brother had landed. He came up coughing and gasping for air. The water was only waist deep but the two thugs were scrambling for their lives. Quickly, they climbed up on the seawall and ran as fast as they could in soaking-wet clothes.

"Don't you fuck with my friend's boat again or I'll kill you bastards!" Doug yelled, as he dropped the anchor's rope.

"Thanks Mark," he said to the muscular man in the sequined dress.

"Doug, its Monique when I'm dressed like this, remember?" the large man said, in as feminine voice as possible.

"Oh yeah, sorry Mar…. I mean Monique. Now where were we?"

****

Frank found a parking spot on the street not far from the entrance of Captain Crabbies. He parked the little car and walked inside the bar. Frank took a seat on one of the stools near the door after putting the Toyota's keys into his front pocket. Madeline came over to see him. She was smiling and in a much better mood now.

"Hi sweetie, I'm glad you came by," Madeline said, touching his hand and setting a drink on the bar in front of him.

"I have a little surprise for you," Frank began. "Now, it's not much and I don't want you to think I went out and bought this especially for you or anything. This is just something I already had and don't need anymore. So I want you to take it, okay?"

"Boy, it sounds lovely, I can hardly wait to see it," Madeline said, rolling her eyes and laughing, having no idea what to expect.

"Could you come outside with me for a second?" Frank asked. Madeline came around the bar and called out to one of the waitresses.

"Vicki, I'll be right back. I'm going outside for just a minute."

"Oooooo!" exclaimed the bar patrons.

Frank took her hand and led Madeline down the sidewalk. When they were close enough, he stopped and pointed to the Toyota sitting under a streetlight. Madeline looked toward the street.

"What?" She said, then her eyes focused. Frank turned her hand over and put the keys to the car in it.

"Frank no. No, I couldn't," she said.

"Madeline it's no big deal, it's yours, take it." He squeezed her hand around the car keys.

"Frank, where did you… I'll pay you whatever you want for it, it'll just take me some time." Madeline was trying not to cry, which would be the second time in as many nights a small cheap car would make her do so.

"You don't owe me anything, you need a car and I happen to have one." Face to face they stood under the street lamp, which cast a romantic glow about Madeline's lovely face. The loud music from the jukebox sounded soft outside on the sidewalk.

"This is the nicest thing anyone has ever done for me." Madeline said trying to hold back the tears.

"That's too bad," Frank said. "You should have nice things done for you all the time." He was looking into Madeline's eyes.

"Maybe after tonight I'll have someone I can do nice things for too?" Madeline said. Her face now was only inches away from Frank's as she whispered the words.

"Maybe?" Frank whispered back.

"Maddy, telephone!" A man with a pool stick in his hand was standing in the doorway of the bar. "Oh, sorry, you want me to tell Vicki to tell them you'll call them back?" Frank now had his hands on his face rubbing his eyes hard. Madeline was at the point where she didn't know if the next sound out of her was going to be a laugh or a cry.

"No, no, I'm coming," she said. Madeline went back inside with Frank following, feeling like someone had just punched him in the stomach.

****

"They've got a couple of guards at the boat. Yeah, we couldn't get on board. A couple real tough guys, we saw one of them out on the boat earlier today with the guy that's intercepting our shipments," Anthony explained to his uncle on the phone. He thought it would be best not to say anything about the guy in the yellow dress kicking their ass.

"This is a bigger ring than we first thought. They've already rubbed out somebody too. I don't know who, but they brought in some muscle today, and he's already killed somebody. Some guy I've never seen before. Must be from the South Miami Cartel, but I saw him take a payoff at the boat a couple hours ago."

"How the fuck do you know it was a hit man?" Eduardo couldn't believe he was having this conversation. "He had a duffel bag with him. It was dripping blood all over the docks. Probably had some wise guy's head in there because he was showing how he choked a guy to death with his bare hands."

****

Frank caught a cab home just before closing time and Madeline took the Toyota. She was going to meet Frank at the boat around ten o'clock tomorrow for the trip to Bimini and she was going to kiss him even if it killed her.

Just after nine o'clock Saturday morning Frank was at Don's shop explaining to him about the suitcase being stolen.

"That's weird. I wonder why they didn't take the money, or the bicycle." Don asked.

"Hell, I don't know. Either they were desperate for a piece of luggage, or they thought there was something valuable in it," Frank answered, shrugging his shoulders. Don pulled another suitcase off a high shelf. Frank guessed people would pawn just about anything for one more night in paradise. Don set the case on the floor behind the counter and began putting the gold objects in it. A newspaper was laying on the counter, the bold type of one of the stories caught Frank's eye. **SUSPECT IN CAR BOMBING RELEASED.** Frank scanned the story. A taxi driver verified the fact that he was taking Bubba, the suspect, home when they heard the explosion. The police investigating the bombing reported the bomb was too large for Bubba to have had with him all evening at the bar. Don set the suitcase on the counter.

"Stop by Monday and we'll see when I need you to

make another run," Don said. Frank picked up the case. It didn't feel as heavy as before.

"Don't feel like there's much in here," he said.

"Dorrey usually has some sent here from other pawn and jewelry shops around Florida. Like the stuff you brought me when we met. I guess thing have been slow," Don said.

"I'll see you Monday." Frank left the shop and headed back to the *Don't Worry* to meet up with Madeline.

CHAPTER 19

Not long after Frank had everything situated on the boat, the Toyota came to a stop in the parking lot. Madeline came walking down the pier in a bright pink sarong with colored flowers. She was wearing a big floppy straw hat and red framed sunglasses covering half her face. She had a cloth handbag, big enough to carry a small television, hanging from her shoulder. "Astronauts could have spotted her from the space shuttle," Frank thought.

"Hey baby," she said in a joking manner as she stepped aboard Frank's boat.

"Well hello beautiful. You look very festive today." Frank said smiling. They kissed hello but it was just a little peck. The mood had to be right for the passionate embrace they were both longing for. Madeline went down into the *Don't Worry's* cabin as Frank launched the little yacht for its voyage from one island to another. He made his way up to the bridge to maneuver out of the marina. Out on the ocean Madeline came up to sit beside him. She had put her things down below and was now in her sunglasses and a white bikini that covered the minimum area that could be covered and still be considered clothed. She looked great with the wind blowing through her hair.

Frank liked having her with him. He had taken the picture of Karen and him off the steering wheel just before Madeline got there, and he was glad he did. He really didn't think she would care, but he didn't want to explain details about why they were no longer together. He knew if they kept seeing each other he would have to, sooner or later, but now was not the time. The water was fairly calm, and the sun was bright as the two of them cruised along not noticing the boat a mile or so behind them. Even if they had, there was nothing unusual about two boats heading for the Bahamas on a Saturday morning.

Once in port at Bimini, Frank and Madeline hailed a cab and headed into town.

"Maybe we could walk back after we're done. Look around a little," Madeline said wrapping her arm around Frank's in the backseat of the cab.

"Sure, that would be nice," Frank answered moving his hand onto Madeline's large thigh. It felt warm from the sun as he gave it a gentle squeeze.

After the short ride they got out at Dorrey's shop. Dorrey seemed a bit concerned that Frank was not alone. He shuffled through the gold, keeping and eye on Madeline. She was looking at some of the more expensive jewelry in the glass cases. Frank could only smile as he watched Madeline bending her large body, now covered by the sarong, over the display cases. She held her hair back with one hand as she looked inside them. He wanted to go over and kiss her, but he had business to tend to first.

When Frank finished with Dorrey, they began their sightseeing walk back to the boat. He soon found out Madeline didn't seem to be able to walk past any shop that appeared to be open. It wasn't long before Frank barely had room in his arms for the suitcase, because of all the things they had purchased for Madeline. He pretended to try and hurry her along, but she knew he was enjoying himself.

They bought wooden figurines to go along with the ones she already had next to her television set. She found some brightly colored dresses that were her size, extra large. Some odds and ends she liked but couldn't justify buying, Frank talked her into letting him buy them for her. She protested but he insisted. She also found a pair of gold hoop earrings in one shop that were the size of coffee can lids. She told Frank she had been looking for a pair like that forever. Frank stopped and looked at her as they left one of the shops.

"Wait a second," he said as he set shopping bag, after shopping bag down on the sidewalk next to the shop's window. Madeline looked at him wondering what was going on.

"What are you doing?" she asked.

"Something I've been trying to do for a long time now," he said, gently pushing her back up against the block wall, and put his lips to hers. Her arms went limp at her side. Frank put his hands on her wide hips. Nothing moved except Frank's head slightly for twenty seconds. Frank finally stepped back, gathered up their bags, and started down the sidewalk toward the docks. After several steps he turned around. Madeline was still leaning against the wall. Frank walked back to where she was. Her eyes were still closed.

"Madeline! Madeline, are you alright?"

"What, oh, yeah I'm okay let's go," she said as she came out of her trance and headed up the sidewalk. This time Frank stayed put.

"Madeline!" he called after her. "The boat is this way honey," nodding his head in the opposite direction. She turned around and walked past Frank like he wasn't there.

They stopped at a small café on the waters edge, not far from the *Don't Worry* for lunch. Frank looked across the table at Madeline in her big floppy hat and sunglasses. She was laughing and talking while taking small bites of her conch salad. The warm wind blew across the small open deck softly blowing her sarong back and forth. For that brief moment life was good again. The feeling faded away as gently as it had come, and they made their way back to Frank's boat.

The crossing back to Key West was nice and peaceful. It was pretty uneventful except when Madeline chose to 'get some sun' and slipped out of her bathing suit. She stretched out across the *Don't Worry's* deck as Frank watched her butt jiggle with each bounce from the waves. He was singing to himself, "Bare Butt Across the Bow of my Boat." As Key West appeared on the horizon, Madeline quickly dressed and took a seat next to Frank. They dropped anchor about a mile out from Key Coast and watched while the sun sank lower and lower in the sky. They held each other close and made up for the lost kisses. After a while they docked the boat and Frank walked Madeline up to her car.

"Why don't you come over in a little while and I'll make dinner," Madeline said softly.

"Mmmm that sounds like a good idea," Frank answered, "about an hour?"

"You'd better give me an hour and a half," Madeline smiled. She got in her little car and drove out of the marina. Frank stood in the parking lot wondering if he was doing the right thing. Karen had only been gone a short while, but he met Madeline now. It's probably too early to start a new relationship, but he can't wait for six months or a year when Madeline was with him today. What about Madeline? Was he using her to erase the pain of his loss? He didn't want to hurt her, and he didn't know how she felt about him. Maybe this was just a fling for her. He didn't think so, but who knew where this was going? Right or wrong he liked Madeline very much. He didn't know why. She wasn't the small petite, laid back, quiet type woman he normally looked for. Not that he was looking, but he sure liked spending time with her.

 Madeline drove the little car Frank had given her down the narrow road to her apartment. Thoughts of giving it back were going through her head. Maybe by taking the car Frank felt like she owed him in some way. She didn't know if she would feel comfortable saying no to him about anything he wanted because of the generous gift. Then again she didn't have a line of guys wanting to date her either. He didn't have to give her a car just to be with her. She liked Frank and would probably do whatever he wanted anyway. She pulled the little Toyota into the shell driveway and parked near the steps of her apartment.

 Two men dressed in black went unnoticed as they slid between the main house and the hibiscus bushes. Anthony waved Paul around the other side to the edge of the garage. By the time they reached the bottom of the stairs Madeline was closing the apartment door behind her.

 She quickly got a few things started in the kitchen then slipped out of the sarong and bikini and jumped in the shower. She never heard the doorknob turn back and forth to see if it was locked. It was.

 Anthony and Paul crept back down the steps and around to the back of the building. A small window appeared to be slightly open to the apartment, but was too high for them to reach.

 Madeline stepped out of the shower, dried quickly, wrapped a towel around her head and went to the kitchen to see how things were progressing. She moved one pan off the burner and set another one on it. She took some vegetables out of the apartment-sized refrigerator and a large salad bowl from the cabinet. A buzzer buzzed and she removed a bowl from the microwave. She took off the towel and rubbed her head vigorously with it and went back into the bathroom. Soon the sound of her blow dryer was filling the night air.

    A padlock hasp, holding shut the side door to Don's garage was ripped away by a steel pipe held by Anthony. Two steps into the dark garage and down he went with a crash, Paul stumbling on top of him.

    The stuff Don didn't have room for in the small pawnshop got stored away in the garage. Not being one to pass up a good deal things got pretty piled up at times. It wasn't a perfect system, but it worked for him.

    "You stupid son of a bitch, what the fuck are you doing?" Anthony said, getting to his feet wanting to yell but trying to keep quiet.

    "Hey it wasn't my fault, this piece of shit was in my way," Paul said, picking up a metal stepladder and throwing it deeper into the dark mangled pile of pawned items. Anthony ran his fingers though his hair to keep from wrapping them around Paul's throat.

    "Two mistakes you just made." Anthony took a deep breath and in a calm voice said, "First; that was aluminum. It makes a lot of noise when you throw it. And secondly, we're looking for a ladder you moron. Now go get it!"

    "Son of a bitch," Paul said, while he fought his way over the lawn mowers, weed eaters, water skis, and other unrecognizable things. Anthony waited by the door, holding up a lighter so Paul could see what he was doing.

    Upstairs Madeline finished her hair and makeup and was at her dresser, still nude picking out her outfit, and feeling good about the evening ahead.

****

Back at the *Don't Worry* Frank showered and changed his clothes. He was having a beer on the deck trying to decide whether to take his bike or catch a cab over to Madeline's apartment.

****

The top of the ladder fell against the back of the garage below the opened window with a light thud. Paul was at the top in no time, but could barely get his hands over the windowsill.

"I need a boost," he said looking back over his shoulder.

"Why am I not surprised?" Anthony said, rolling his eyes and went up the ladder behind his younger brother to assist.

Madeline was turning around in front of a full-length mirror attached to her closet door. She was admiring the bright, thin fabric of the sundress Frank had picked out for her while they were in Bimini. The large hoop earrings dangled lightly against her neck as she spun around in her highest high heels. She froze solid and stared hard into the mirror. Grabbing at the dress hand full after hand full, inching the hem up past her knee and along her thigh until the red satin of her panties were slightly exposed. The color matched that of her shoes and bra. She looked at herself in the mirror and smiled until it turned into a laugh. It was going to be an unforgettable night.

CHAPTER 20

Frank decided it would be best to take a cab so he wouldn't be hot and sweaty from the bike ride when he arrived. Not that it mattered; sweat was a way of life in Key West. If he was going to give her a hug and kiss when he said good night, he thought taking a cab would be the better choice.

****

Paul fell from the window onto Madeline's floor. He got to his feet as quickly as he could, but not before Madeline let out a scream and planted her knee into his face. He stumbled forward, grabbing a hold of her left arm just long enough to get punched in the stomach by her right fist. She stood between him and the door.
 A tall crystal bud vase was sitting in the middle of a lovely table for two with a pink silk rose placed in it. Desperate now with blood dripping from his nose, Paul grabbed the vase and raised it up over his head. Madeline backed away when Paul lunged toward her. She cautiously moved away from the door. As he reached for the lock, Madeline thought she had scared him off and he was

leaving. This thought faded quickly when the lock clicked, and Anthony burst though the door with a roll of duct tape in his hand. Before Madeline knew what was happening, he had taped her mouth shut and the two men pinned her to the floor. After securing her hands behind her back they led her down the stairway, though the bushes to their pickup truck.

"Get your ass in there," Paul said as he pushed Madeline into the cab of the truck, and then got in beside her. Anthony started the engine and spun the tires down the narrow lane.

Frank glanced at his watch; it was about time for him to get going. He went down into the *Don't Worry's* cabin to find a shirt. He was fastening the buttons on one of his favorite Hawaiian style shirts while coming back up the steps, when the barrel of a gun was pushed into his temple.

"Where's all the coke asshole?" Anthony's hand was steady.

"It's in the refrigerator," Frank said wondering what the hell was going on, raising his hands slightly to show he was unarmed.

"You got forty kilos of coke in the refrigerator?" Anthony mocked.

"No, just a six pack, I think there's four cans left." Frank answered.

"Shut up smart ass." The butt of the gun came down hard against the back of his head. Frank dropped to his knees. He saw tiny silver spots floating in circles before his eyes, as he shook his head. "Who is this guy and what the hell is he talking about?" Frank thought. Anthony went down into the cabin for just a few seconds then returned.

"Where's the cocaine asshole!" Anthony yelled.

"Cocaine, I don't know anything about any cocaine."

Frank thought that's probably the same thing someone would say even if they did know something about the cocaine.

"Get up you fucking scumbag." Anthony said, grabbing a hold of Frank by the pit of his arm and pulling him to his feet.

"Let's go asshole. You were a lot easier than the guy in that stupid looking dress."

"Madeline! You've got Madeline! Who are you? What do you want?" Frank was no longer afraid. Now he was mad, and more worried about Madeline than he was for himself, which he found odd.

"Is that what you call that freak? That guy almost killed my brother." Anthony shoved Frank in the pickup and got in behind him. "Don't tell me you care for that freak?"

Frank felt the anger starting to boil inside him. He didn't like to hear Madeline being called a freak. He lowered his head remembering how he had thought she was a man at one time himself. There was nothing he could do. He couldn't fight back even if he wanted to since he knew they had her.

"Yeah, yeah I do," he said looking at the floorboard of the truck, saying it to himself more than to the thug driving.

****

After a few funny twists and turns the truck stopped in an ally next to some dumpsters. Anthony jerked Frank out of the truck and banged the gun against a metal door with flaking gray paint. There were other doors just like it along the wall of the ally. They were at the rear entrances to store's in a strip mall.

After a short wait, Paul opened the door and Frank

was shoved inside. It had been a clothing shop at one time, but had been sitting empty for several months. There were clothes racks scattered haphazardly about. The walls were filled with shelves and wire hooks to hang clothing from. The glass storefront was covered with newspapers to keep the people walking by on the sidewalk from looking in. Some of the paper had fallen and lay on the dusty floor, letting just enough light in from the streetlamps to be able to find your way around.

In the middle of the room, sitting on an office chair that was missing one of its wheels, was Madeline. She looked calm to Frank as she stared at the floor.

"Alright you mother fuckers, I want to know what you did with the shipment of cocaine you picked up in Bimini?" Frank looked at Madeline.

"What cocaine? We didn't pick up cocaine, we dropped off jewelry," Frank answered feeling responsible for putting Madeline in this predicament. Anthony shook his head and was waving the gun around.

"Jewelry! Jewelry! Do you think I'm some kind of an idiot?" He turned to Paul. "Search that fucking fag." He pointed the gun at Madeline. Paul stood in front of her in the dim light.

"Stand up you old drag queen!" He spoke louder than necessary. Madeline rose gracefully. Frank noticed for the first time that her hands were bound behind her back. Paul clicked open a large knife and placed it between Madeline's bare shoulder and her dress. The light from outside reflected off the chrome blade as it cut through the light fabric. He then repeated the process on the other shoulder. Her beautiful dress hit the dirty floor.

"Step out of the dress you homo," Paul said. Madeline stepped out of the mound of cloth around her ankles and sat back down in the chair, carefully so not to tip it over. Paul bent down and picked up the garment. After several sounds of the knife slicing through the floral patterned cloth he lifted it into the light.

"There ain't nothing here man," he said holding up the shredded dress while standing over Madeline, looking at his brother. Madeline planted her shiny red high heel deep into his groin.

"You son of a bitch that was a brand new dress!" she yelled. Paul dropped the knife and grabbed for his crotch. He fell to his knees.

"Oh, my nuts," he moaned before ending up in the fetal position on the floor. A small dust cloud rose up around him.

"What the fuck?" Anthony lowered the gun and went to the aid of his fallen brother. Frank slowly moved toward the knife. When Anthony bent over to see to Paul, Frank grabbed it and shoved it hard into the back of Anthony's thigh.

"My leg!" he screamed. As the thug turned, Frank swung the knife at the hand that was raising the gun. It cut into his forearm somewhere near Anthony's wrist. Anthony dropped the weapon and grabbed the open wound with his other hand. He backed away from the gun as Frank came closer wielding the knife. Frank picked up the pistol as Madeline ran over to him. She turned around so he could cut the duct tape from her wrist. Once she was free the two of them ran out the door as the thugs struggled to get to their feet. Frank threw the weapons into the dumpster as they ran past it and headed up the ally. Madeline's high-heeled shoes sounded like horse hooves clicking on the pavement.

"We're not far from my place," Madeline said, as they turned onto a side street.

"We can't go back there. That would be the first place they'll look for us," Frank said, taking a hand.

"But I need some clothes," she whined.

"We don't have time for that," Frank said. Madeline pulled her hand loose from his and stopped.

"I'm not about to start running all over town in my underwear." Frank started to unbutton his shirt and offer it to her until she stopped him.

"And what am I supposed to do with that?" Madeline said, placing her hands on her hips. Frank realized that with her size, his shirt was useless. Just then, headlights came out of the alley. This time Madeline grabbed Frank's hand and took off up the street. They ducked around the corner and hid in the doorway of a small art gallery closed up for the night. Frank quietly watched as the black Chevy slowly drove past, its passenger hanging out the window.

"We need to try and get to the boat," he said, "so we can get out of town."

"Okay," Madeline agreed, but was unhappy about the situation.

They skirted along side streets as long as they could, but the last few blocks were going to be down busy Duval Street. Frank turned to Madeline as they hid in the shadows.

"I'm sorry about this," Frank said.

"I was planning on you seeing me in this tonight, but not the whole town," Madeline said, referring to her satin undergarments. She hung her head.

"You look beautiful," Frank touched her cheek. He meant what he said. She really did look beautiful.

"Well, are you ready to go?" Before Frank finished the question Madeline was ten strides down Duval. Frank took off after her but was losing ground with every step.

Normally a six-foot tall redhead clad only in red shoes, panties, and bra running down a city street would cause quite a reaction, but it was business as usual along Duval.

Things were hopping at the Island Breeze bar as Madeline approached. The tables at the open-air bar sat right out on the sidewalk. She hoped no one decided to push out his or her chair as she ran past or a collision was bound to happen.

The flash of skin and satin made it though without a hitch. A man sitting at one of the tables, who may have had one too many beers, leaned over in his seat. He stopped his drinking long enough to watch the near nude woman run down the street. Frank passed by a few seconds later.

"You go get her boy!" Wally yelled, not recognizing Frank. "I'll get the next one that comes along," he said into his beer, then taking a swallow. After setting the cold beer down on the table he spoke to no one in particular, but loud enough for everyone to hear.

"I knew those stories were true.... I fucking knew they were."

Madeline got past the part she dreaded the most and was coming up to the water's edge of the small harbor. Key Coast Marina lay just to the east, with Mallory Square to the west. Madeline stopped in the shadows next to a car parked under a palm tree to let Frank catch up. Once they caught their breath, they walked toward the marina, still hiding in the shadows. Peering out over the water they could see the black truck from hell slide into the parking lot at Key Coast.

"Now what are we going to do Frank? I'm not going back up Duval Street dressed like this," Madeline said, with a slight whimper.

"Don't worry; everything is going to be fine. Come on." he said, wishing he believed it. He took her by the hand and headed in the opposite direction from the marina. Frank led Madeline along the water's edge until they came up on Mallory Square. Across the open area was a restaurant and souvenir shop.

"Can you swim?" Frank asked. Madeline nodded her

head. "If we can make it to that restaurant, we can swim across the bay to the boat without them seeing us." He looked at Madeline. She didn't say anything. "Well?" he said.

"Well what? It's not like I have a lot of choices you know." She let out a nervous laugh. Frank put his arms around her. She laid her head on his shoulder for a brief second.

"Everything is going to be okay," he said. She nodded again. "When I say go, you take off running and I'll be right behind you," Frank said. Another nod came from the redhead. "Okay, let's go!"

A small group of tourists had gathered nearby watching as a street performer poured a pitcher of milk into a cone made out of a rolled-up newspaper. As Madeline made her dash across the square, the crowd watching started applauding when they saw her. In her skimpy bright red outfit they thought she must be part of the magicians act. The hooting, hollering, and hand clapping quickly quieted down when they saw she wasn't stopping to assist with the trick. They watched as the near-nude woman did her own magic trick by disappearing behind the building with Frank close behind her. She dropped to the ground in the darkness. Frank fell to his knees beside her.

"Are you alright?" he asked.

"As well as can be expected, I guess," she answered.

From where they sat Frank could see a little bit of what was going on at Key Coast. A lone streetlamp was all that lit up the marina. He could see Paul leaning against the black Chevy with a rifle in his hands. Anthony's outline was walking around down by the boat docks. The end of his cigarette glowed orange in the darkness as he inhaled.

Frank and Madeline climbed down the seawall and into the knee-deep water. It was slightly cooler than the air and felt good against their sweaty skin. Slowly they waded deeper and deeper. Now with the water up to Frank's chest and just past Madeline's navel, he motioned his head toward the boat. Madeline had a strong stroke and was in front of him in no time.

Pink and blue neon lights from the surrounding businesses danced off the water's dark surface as they quietly crossed the inlet. Music was playing off in the distance at a much happier place, where a woman wasn't swimming in her underwear toward two men with guns. After the short swim they were soon back in waist deep water with just the *Don't Worry* and dock between them and the gunmen. Frank leaned against the stern of the boat. This wasn't what he came to Key West for. All he wanted to do was sit in the sun, drinking margaritas, like in the Johnny Branson songs. Not start a war with Cuba, or whoever these assholes were.

"You stay here, I'll be right back," he whispered to Madeline between heavy breaths. Her perfectly applied makeup was now just a mess of dark streaks running down her pretty face. Frank eased between the wooden post of the dock and the *Don't Worry*. He waited until Anthony had walked past before reaching up and untying the rope from the cleat on the dock. Then he waded around to the other side of the boat and waited under the dock until Anthony was clear again. He removed the rope from its anchored location. Near the seawall Frank spotted an empty beer can afloat. Grabbing the can he went back to the rear of the boat where he had left Madeline. She was still there but starting to cry.

"Madeline, sweetheart its okay, we're almost out of this mess," Frank said, pushing some of her wet hair away from her face. She stopped crying almost instantly.

"What did you just call me?" she asked. Frank looked her in the eyes.

"What?"

"Did you just call me sweetheart?"

"Um, um I might of, I don't know, if I did I didn't mean to?" Frank was lost; this was not a good time to be dissecting sentences.

"Why are you with me Frank?" Frank put his head against the out drive of the engine. He was waist deep in water, in the dark, with two goons carrying guns looking for him, and the only person on his side was a woman in her underwear, and now she wanted to get psychological with him. He thought for a second. By the look on Madeline's face he could see she wasn't moving one inch until she got an answer, and it had better be the right one. This was life or death, if he pissed her off now, it could get bloody.

Frank was never one to play games or beat around the bush when it came to his feelings. Before his head could figure out if this was one of those times in a guy's life when he is supposed to lie to a woman, his heart said how he really felt.

"Because I love Key West, and you are Key West to me," Frank put his face in his hands. What the hell did he just say? "Your Key West to me....." What the hell is that supposed mean and how big of a cornball do you have to be to say it? He thought.

"Oh Frank, really? That's the sweetest thing anyone has ever said to me." Madeline put her arms around his neck; they were almost touching nose to nose. Frank wanted to answer but was not sure what he said, or if it made the slightest bit of sense.

"Madeline we need to get a move on." He said it as romantically as it could be said, under the circumstances.

"You're right, we do. Let's go," Madeline said, still looking into Frank's eyes. Finally releasing her embrace she was back to the task at hand.

Frank filled the beer can with seawater and peeked around the corner of the boat to see where Anthony and Paul were. Paul was still at the truck and Anthony had his back to them. Madeline waded around the engines propeller to the other side and took a hold of the boat. Slowly, they began pulling the *Don't Worry* out of its slip. Their feet sank into the sandy ocean floor. Frank was keeping and eye on Anthony the whole time. When the little yacht was half-way out of the slip, Anthony started to turn around. Frank threw the beer car as far as he could toward the other side of their truck. Anthony raised the pistol and ran in Paul's direction. Paul fired a shot at who-knows-what. Frank heard the bullet zinging toward the open ocean.

"What the fuck are you shooting at, you moron?" Anthony screamed.

"I...I don't know, I thought I saw that guy in the yellow dress again," Paul said looking around.

"You could have killed me you dumb ass!" Anthony said walking up toward the truck.

The bow of the *Don't Worry* just cleared the dock. Frank and Madeline stopped pulling and started pushing. They turned the boat's nose toward the open sea. Once past the open slip, and with another boat between them and the two men yelling at each other, Frank and Madeline climbed aboard. Frank scrambled quickly up the ladder to get the engines started and head for safety.

CHAPTER 21

Out on the open ocean at night gives a person a powerful feeling of freedom. Frank was feeling it now more than ever as the small marina slipped out of sight. Madeline came up on the bridge wrapped in a blanket.

"I hope you don't mind?" she asked. Frank shook his head.

"Where are we going?"

"I'm not sure. We'll stay somewhere in the Keys until we find out what the hell is going on, but I don't think Key West is safe for us right now." Madeline agreed and settled into the seat next to Frank.

According to the *Don't Worry's* global positioning system they were just off the coast of Big Pine Key when Frank dropped anchor.

"We'll spend the night out here, and in the morning we can go ashore and see what we can find out about those assholes chasing us," Frank said. He looked around to make sure no one was coming from all directions.

"Aye aye captain, whatever you say." Madeline answered with a playful salute. It was an odd time for a sense of humor but Frank found himself smiling at her.

They went into the cabin but found it difficult to sleep.

After dozing off a half a dozen times the sun was coming up. Frank wanted to find a place to dock a little out of the way for safety's sake. After cruising along the coastline for a short distance, he spotted a seaside restaurant with a pier across the back for boating customers. The restaurant was closed and didn't open until eleven o'clock for lunch. Frank tied off the boat and went to wake up Madeline. He had forgotten she didn't have anything to wear until he saw the red under garments hanging from one of the cabinet knobs. She was awake, still wearing the blanket like a sleeveless dress. She was seated on the edge of the sofa area that had been converted into a bed for her.

"Good morning," she said sleepily, rubbing her eyes with her fingers. Frank didn't know what to say knowing she had nothing to put on so they could go into town.

"I found a place to dock," he said. Madeline pulled the blanket away from her chest just enough for her to peek inside, to see if this had been a bad dream or not. She saw there was nothing under it but her, so it must be true.

"What am I suppose to do? I don't have any clothes, I don't have any money, I don't know how far from home I am, no make up, not even a damn hair brush." God she was beautiful sitting there wrapped in the blanket complaining, Frank thought.

"Well, tell me what you need and I'll go and get it for you." Madeline stood up and waddled like a duck wrapped in the blanket across the small cabin floor. She took a notepad off a shelf where Frank had some nautical maps, a couple magazines, and a book or two. She wrote something on the notepad, tore the page off, and handed it to Frank.

"Here, you can find this in the men's section. This will get me by for now," she said.

Frank put the note in his shirt pocket without looking at it, feeling a little guilty he had a shirt.

"I'll be back as quickly as I can," he said. Madeline opened the side of her makeshift robe exposing her bare side to him.

"I'm not going any place," she said, half joking, half pissed off.

Frank lifted his bike off the boat and rode up A1A until he found a department store. As he was making his way to the men's section he felt bad for Madeline having to wear men's clothes, knowing that she preferred to dress so much like a lady. She must not have had enough confidence in Frank to trust him in the ladies section, or maybe she thought it would embarrass him to buy a dress and a pair of women's shoes. Frank saw a young lady standing at a makeup counter in the center of the store looking somewhat bored. This gave him an ideal.

"Excuse me miss?" he began. "My wife is back in the hotel and she has left her makeup case at home. I was wondering if you could put a few things together for her. I can't get her to come out of our room without her makeup on."

The young woman's eyes brightened. Frank didn't know if it was from joy of putting together a whole makeup kit or the thought of the commission she would receive in her paycheck.

"She needs everything. A brush, eye liner whatever you can think of," Frank said.

"Sure, sure I can put something together for you."

"Thank you, I have some other things I need to pick up, I'll be back in a few minutes." Frank left her to her task and headed for the men's clothing section. He took the note out of his pocket to look at it for the first time. Madeline had written down the sizes for a pair of shorts, T-shirt, and a pair of tennis shoes. Frank picked out the colors he thought would look best on Madeline. He found a pair of dark blue walking shorts and a light gray T-shirt.

There was one thing he knew about picking out clothing for a woman. No matter how hard he tried to get it right, chances were good that he would be wrong.

When he got back to the makeup counter the girl had a pile of tiny bottles, jars, plastic boxes, and hair care products. Some little metal device that looked like it was invented to torture people by pulling out their toe nails, and some other thing that were in packages that Frank couldn't identify. The girl saw Frank coming up the aisle and hung her head feeling maybe she had over done it.

"Is that everything?" Frank asked. With that she cheered up again.

"She'll be as beautiful as the day you married her," the sales girl said.

Frank felt his heart skip a beat knowing the only woman he had ever even thought of marrying had been Karen.

"I can ring everything up for you right here," she said taking the clothes from Frank.

"Are you sure you got the right size here," she said holding up the shorts and looking at Frank. "These are going to be awful big on you."

"What, oh, yeah I like them to fit a little loose," Frank answered, just wanting to get out of the store. When the girl finally finished, his receipt was over two feet long. He paid the young woman and left the store feeling a little sad that he had bought these things for someone other than Karen.

When Frank got back to the boat Madeline was just stepping out of the shower. He handed her the clothing he had bought though the small door.

"Where are we?" she asked from inside the bathroom.

"We're docked at a restaurant on Big Pine Key," Frank answered. She stepped out into the main cabin wearing the new shorts and T-shirt.

"Not too bad, I guess I'm good to go," she said striking a pose somewhat pleased with the outfit. Frank handed her the bag of cosmetics the sales girl had prepared for him.

"Oh Frank, thank you, you're so thoughtful." She put her arms around him and kissed him on the cheek.

"There's a pay phone in front of the restaurant. I'm going to call Key Coast and see if they know what the hell is going on. When I get back we'll figure out what we're going to do next," Frank said. Madeline began sorting though the beauty items. He walked around to the front of the restaurant to the phone.

"Hello Key Coast Marina," Doug answered.

"Doug, this is Frank, has anybody been by there looking for me?" Frank said, watching cars pass by on A1A.

"Well yeah, like the whole damn town." Doug said, in the smart-ass tone that Frank had found funny before, but was just aggravating now.

"What do you mean the whole town? Like who?" Frank asked.

"Well, let's see, first two good looking studs in tight jeans came by asking where your boat was." Frank rolled his eyes, if he could just keep from puking. "I told them that I was not your babysitter so how should I know?" Doug paused to laugh at his own joke. "Then some red neck guy stopped in looking for you," Doug continued. "Oh, oh and here was the funny one. A couple guys pulled up in a pickup with a Magic Wizard boat repair sign on the door, one of those magnetic ones. I saw them get out and walk down to where you were docked and look around, then they left. They may have been the same guys that were in here looking for you earlier, but I couldn't tell for sure. They were too far away." Doug was making hand gestures as if Frank could see him.

"You didn't get the phone number off the truck did

you?" Frank asked.

"Yes, as a matter of fact I did. I even dialed it to see if they were based in Key West," Doug said, still waving his hands about. "The number was out of service. Hey, hang on I think your redneck friend is back. He's coming across the parking lot."

"Redneck, what redneck?" Frank asked

"I don't know, how many redneck friends do you have? To tell you the truth I think you'd be better off with the tall one in the black jeans." Doug was trying to be funny now. Frank heard Doug talking to someone while he had his hand over the receiver.

"He says his name is Wally," Doug said into the phone.

"Oh thank God, Wally. Let me talk to him," Frank said. Doug handed the phone over to Wally with the instruction to not spit that shit on the floor; he would find him a cup.

"Hello?" Wally said.

"Hey Wally, it's me, Frank. I need your help again. I think somebody thinks I'm running cocaine and they're trying to kill me. I'm at Big Pine Key at…" Frank looked up at the sign on the front of the restaurant. "Sandy Sam's Seaside Café. Could you bring the Toyota up here. I can't come back to Key West in the boat because they're looking for it." Frank said hoping Wally wasn't in a hurry to get back to Crystal River.

"Why don't you go to the police?" Wally said. He covered the phone with his hand and turned to Doug.

"Thanks," he said followed by a spitting sound.

"We're going to go to the police as soon as we get back to Key West. We just found out they're trying to kill us last night and had to get out of town as fast as we could." Frank said.

"Did you say we or me?" Wally asked.

"Oh, I have a lady friend with me," Frank answered.

"Well first of all I don't know where the Toyota is, and secondly, what kind of lady friend?" Wally said. Madeline came around the corner of the restaurant and Frank waved her over to where he was.

"Wally, the car is at her place." Frank asked Madeline for her address then repeated it into the phone. It's around back. Ask for Don at the house. I'll call him and tell him you're coming and he can let you in her apartment." He broke off to ask Madeline where the car keys were. "The keys are on the kitchen counter. Okay." Frank heard Wally and Doug talking back and forth.

"Hey Frank, the little guy here at the marina says he knows where Don lives and where Sandy Sam's Seaside Cafe on Big Pine Key is. Would it be alright if he comes along?" Wally asked. Frank wondered if Wally knew Doug was gay.

"Sure, I guess so, I don't care," Frank said.

"He says we should be there in about an hour." Wally said, and then he spit.

"Okay buddy I'll see you then," Frank said, as he hung up the phone.

"Who was that?" Madeline asked.

"Wally. He's a friend of mine. He and Doug are going to come and get us," Frank said.

"You mean Doug, from the marina?" Madeline asked.

"Yeah, Doug from the marina, and Wally," Frank answered.

"And who's this Wally person?" Madeline said, twirling her hair.

"He's a guy I met last week. He's kind of a redneck," Frank said, using Doug's description for lack of a better one, and finding it hard to say with much confidence. Madeline looked out across A1A.

"We're depending on a gay guy and a redneck to come

and get us?" she asked.

"Yep," Frank answered; Madeline looked down at the ground and gently kicked at a small rock with her new tennis shoe.

"It's gonna be a long day isn't it?" Madeline squinted her eyes in the bright sun. Frank paused.

"Yep," he said, starting to have second thoughts.

"You don't think they'll try to kill each other, do you?" Madeline asked. Frank thought for a moment.

"Well, if they do I hope they do it after they get here." Frank lifted the receiver from the pay phone and called Don. He had just got back from Key Largo to pick up some gold that Dorrey needed. Don said he would help in anyway he could and was worried about Madeline. She talked with him for a minute to let him know she was all right. After she hung up with Don she called her boss at Captain Crabbies to let him know she wouldn't be in for a day or two.

After finishing their phone calls they crossed the street to a donut shop for some breakfast. When they got back to the restaurant it wasn't long before the little Toyota came into view and pulled into the parking area.

"Oh boy, are we ever glad to see you guys," Frank said, as the two men got out of the car. Doug was wearing a light purple tank top, dark purple bicycle shorts, and a yellow sweatband around his head. Wally had on a pair of faded jeans and an old Dan Marino football jersey that had pieces of the number thirteen peeling off of it. Only in the Keys was Wally the one that looked out of place.

"First of all we need to find a place where I can dock my boat for a few days. Then I want to go back to Key West and contact the police there," Frank said, leaning against the little car.

"Hey my dad has a friend," Doug said, slowly looking around like he was trying to figure out exactly where he was. "He lives here on Big Pine on a canal someplace. He has a boat dock, but he doesn't own a boat."

Doug took his cell phone out of the waistband of his shorts. He called his father and got a phone number, then called his father's friend. Frank introduced Madeline to Wally. Wally looked Madeline up and down like he was trying to place where he might have seen her before.

"I think I might have seen you someplace before." he said.

"I work at Captain Crabbies. Maybe you've seen me in there. Madeline replied.

"No, that's not it, but I know I've seen you somewhere." Wally was trying to recall where it was.

"Okay I've got it. We're all set and it's not that far from here," Doug said, putting the phone back in his waistband. He told Wally how to get there in the car and he boarded the boat with Madeline and Frank.

During the boat ride, Doug told Frank about the two guys that he and his friend had run off the night before near Frank's boat. He wasn't sure, but he thought they were the same guys who were at the marina looking for him that morning.

After getting the *Don't Worry* safely stored away, they loaded up in the cramped little car and headed back across the bridge toward Key West.

CHAPTER 22

Soon the foursome was entering the office of the Key West police station. Quinn Ackers was sitting behind her desk typing on a computer.

"Is there something I can do for you folks?" she said, as if it upset her that they had interrupted her typing.

"Yes, someone is trying to kill us. We were abducted last night but we were able to escape," Frank began. "They're trying to hunt us down because they think we're smuggling cocaine."

"I see, so you're a drug runner and you want us to protect you from your boss. Is that what you're saying?" she said it like she had heard this all before.

"No!" Frank exclaimed. "I'm not a drug runner, but some guys are after..." Quinn butted in.

"You're from out of town aren't you?" she said, looking over the top of her glasses.

"Fill out this form please," she handed him a piece of paper.

"Look, is there someone I can report this to?" Frank asked.

"Report what." The lady looked at Frank like he was speaking a foreign language, tilting her head to one side.

"That we were abducted and are being chased by a couple of guys with guns," Frank was trying to keep his cool.

"Oh come on now, drug smuggling, guys chasing you, kidnappers?" Quinn began. "Look we get tourists in here all the time because they thought they saw a pirate on the balcony of their hotel, or that the island is sinking because they marked the waters edge with a stick yesterday and now it's gone. Just because Key West isn't as exiting as your travel agent made it sound, don't try and add a little island mystery to your vacation at our expense, alright?"

Madeline stepped in, "look lady, is there someone here with a brain that we could talk to?" Quinn pretended to take offense, but it was already obvious that she was not going to help for some unknown reason.

"Just fill out this form, with your address and I will file it. When we get more information, we will get in touch with you," Quinn said pushing the form toward Madeline. Madeline took the form, wadded it up and threw it at the woman.

"Tell me how you're going to get in touch with me, if I can't go home without being attacked, you stupid bitch?" Madeline stomped out of the station. Frank, Wally, and Doug had no choice but to follow the large woman out the door.

"That went well didn't it?" Doug said once the men were outside.

"Did anybody see which way Hurricane Madeline went?" Frank asked.

"She's over by the car. We should probably get there before she tries to run it through the police station," Wally said, pointing toward the Toyota. Frank couldn't believe they were making jokes, but it was the only way they knew to lift the tension. Doug and Wally leaned against the little car while Madeline calmed down and Frank thought of what to do next.

"Wally, I want you to drop us off at Madeline's apartment," Frank said. "Then, I want you and Doug to go to the Marina and see if those guys are still hanging around down there. Meet us at Don Gold and Pawn when you finish, okay?"

"Whatever you say Frank," Wally said and got in behind the wheel.

Wally and Doug dropped them off and headed for Key Coast. Frank quietly slipped up the stairs to Madeline's apartment. He didn't know if anyone would be around or not, but he didn't want to take any chances. The door was unlocked, and no one was inside. Madeline came up the steps behind him holding onto the back of his shirt.

"Gather up some clothes and stuff and we'll get a hotel room somewhere for a few nights," Frank said. Madeline didn't hesitate as she hurried past him and pulled a travel bag out from under the bed and began packing dresses, shoes, tops, shorts and a half dozen other things. Frank looked over the perfectly set table for two, minus the bud vase. He saw the spoiled half prepared food on the counter. Candles and a book of matches were lying on the small coffee table. The radio was set on a light jazz station and was playing at a very low volume. Frank thought back to the sexy lingerie that Madeline had been wearing last night. He thought a lot of her but he didn't know if he was ready for what she had in mind. He also didn't think he would be strong enough to stop her if things got started, at least not without getting physically harmed. Frank knew she had every right to feel the way she did. After all they have been spending a lot of time together. They had kissed passionately more than once. Under any other circumstances he would have been ready for the same thing, but not now, not this soon. Would he lose her if he tried to slow down the relationship? As much as he hated the thought of it, he would just have to lose her.

****

The Toyota pulled over to the curb a block away from the marina. Doug and Wally sat in the car and watched the two men sitting in the black pickup.

"This is kind of dumb," Wally said. "Why are we hiding from them? They don't know who the hell we are. They're after Frank."

"Well then tough guy, walk over there and ask them if they want to play a game of tennis with us," Doug answered letting Wally know he wasn't going to walk up to them. Wally spit out the window.

"We'll both go." Wally wasn't asking. "Come on."

Wally and Doug got out of the car at the same time and began to approach the pickup from behind. Paul had one foot up on the dashboard and was cleaning his fingernails with a knife He sat up quickly when he saw the man dressed in purple walking toward them in the side mirror.

"Anthony, that guy that attacked you with the boat anchor, he's coming up behind us." Paul said with fear in his voice. Anthony looked through the back glass and saw Wally, the hit man they had seen at the boat yesterday.

"Oh shit, hang on," Anthony said. He started up the truck and took off like a madman. Wally and Doug stood in the dust left behind by their spinning tires.

"What the hell did they do that for?" Wally replied. Doug shrugged his shoulders.

"I don't know. I'll wait here, you take my cell phone, and if they come back, I'll call you guys," Doug said holding out his phone. Wally took the cell phone and headed for the pawnshop.

Frank put Madeline's suitcase in the trunk of the cab and told the driver to take them to Don's shop. Madeline

cuddled up against Frank in the backseat.
    They couldn't believe their eyes when they arrived at Don's. The windows were smashed to bits, and crime scene tape was stretched across the front entrance of the shop. Don had a moving truck parked on the street, and was pushing a lawn mower up into the back of it when the cab stopped.
    "What the hell happened here?" Frank said, as Madeline was getting her piece of luggage out of the trunk and paying the driver.
    "Hell if I know," Don said. "It's the strangest thing I've ever seen. They didn't take anything." He shrugged his shoulders. "The cops said it was probably some kids down here on vacation. It happened last night. They were just being mean, I guess." Don walked back down the ramp of the truck. Wally pulled up in the Toyota a few minutes later. Frank introduced him to Don.
    "Hey, by the way Frank, could you make another run to the Bahamas tomorrow? Dorrey had me pick up some stuff in Key Largo," Don asked, while pushing a bicycle toward the rental truck.
    "Well, yeah, I guess so." Frank said, a little surprised that Don was as calm as he was. Frank and Wally helped Don load some of the stuff on the truck. Don talked about early retirement or maybe moving to Miami and reopening.
    Madeline took the Toyota and went to Captain Crabbies to reschedule her hours and pick up some sandwiches for everyone. Once the truck was full, they told Don where they would be staying, so if for some reason he needed to get in touch with them he could. Frank drove as they headed to the hotel where Wally had rented a room.
    "What's this about you making some kind of run for that guy?" Wally asked as they drove along.

"He has some kind of a deal with a guy in Bimini, over in the Bahamas. They ship gold jewelry over there and sell it to the tourists as souvenirs," Frank answered, while Wally just nodded.

"How much stuff does he send over each time?" Wally asked, looking for someplace to spit.

"Not very much, it all fits in a suitcase," Frank answered. "He pays me two hundred and fifty dollars a trip." Wally rubbed his chin.

"Why doesn't he just mail it over there?" Frank had never thought of that. It did seem a little crazy to pay so much to have it taken by boat.

"That's a good question, I don't know." Frank's voice trailed off as he was trying to think. He had checked everything out. He was sure there were no drugs in the suitcase, and Don certainly wasn't the type of person to be involved in anything shady. Frank knew that now that he had gotten to know Don.

Madeline stepped into the conversation. "Don wouldn't have Frank do anything illegal. He's a very honest man." She wasn't about to let anyone talk bad about her friend.

"I don't doubt that, but maybe Don doesn't know the whole story. Maybe they're using Don, and the jewelry business as some sort of front for something else," Wally leaned forward in the back seat. "Hey, by the way could we stop by the bus station? I need to be heading out in the morning." Madeline gave Frank directions to the bus station as they drove along.

"That must be why they ripped your dress off, Madeline," Frank said starting to put things together in his head. "They thought you had their cocaine."

"They did what?" Wally said hoping the conversation would take a new direction. Frank's head was spinning when they pulling into the bus depot. Wally and Frank went inside to get the ticket.

"I just don't see how, I've checked out the luggage, it's clean. I already thought of that," Frank said, as they waited in line.

"Maybe they're not sending it in the case. Maybe they're hiding it aboard the *Don't Worry* somewhere. Besides you wouldn't ship it from Key West, you would ship it to Key West wouldn't you?" Wally said and then stepped outside the bus depot to spit.

"Son of a bitch! I never thought of that," Frank said. "How could it get on and off the boat without me knowing?"

"I don't know, it's just a thought," Wally said. After they got the bus ticket to Crystal River, Frank and Madeline got a room with separate beds at the hotel.

****

Anthony and Paul were in their own hotel room on the other side of town. Anthony kept peeking out the window to make sure the hit man hadn't followed them.

"Hey, look at this," Paul said, tossing the newspaper down on the table in front of his older brother. **"Pawnshop vandalized by vacationing teens."** Read the headline.

"Mother fucker!" Anthony was furious. All he wanted to do was nail these bastards and get back to Miami. Just a simple little back off or I'll kill your stupid asses and he would have been done. By now he should have been relaxing in South Beach, drinking margaritas and be surrounded by topless women, while his uncle was singing his praises among the southern Florida under-world elite. But no, life couldn't be that sweet. They have a hit man after them. A couple of freaks guarding the boat tossed them into the ocean. Some drag queen in satin panties almost castrated Paul with a high heel shoe. Now this, one crime family destroys the headquarters of another's and the fucking cops pin it on a bunch of high school pranksters. This is the kind of shit that could ruin the cocaine business. Where is the respect? Where is the credit he deserves?

****

    That evening at the hotel Frank came up with a plan. He called Key Coast while Madeline was in the shower.
    "Hello is Doug there?"
    "No sir he's not. He went out for the evening," the voice on the other end of the line answered.
    "Can you tell me where I might find him?" Frank asked.
    "Well, he usually goes to The Pink Pirate if he doesn't have a date," the man's voice said, Frank figured it was Doug's father.
    "Okay thank you," Frank said and hung up the phone. Someone was knocking on the hotel room door.
    "Who is it?" Frank asked.
    "It's me, Wally," the voice outside the door answered. Frank let him in as Madeline was coming out of the bathroom already dressed.
    "Do you know where a bar named The Pink Pirate is?" Frank asked her.
    "What do you want to know that for?" she asked. Wally started to laugh.
    "That sounds like a gay bar or something," he said. Frank looked at Wally.
    "It is, I'm looking for Doug," Frank answered.
    "What would Doug be doing at a gay bar?" Wally asked, still laughing. Frank looked at Madeline as she turned and took a step toward Wally.
    "Doug's gay dear," Madeline said.

"Gee Madeline; you didn't have to be so straight forward." Frank put his hand on her arm. Wally stopped laughing. He looked dumbfounded.

"Nooo.... Really.... Nooo.... Doug, really.... Nooo?" Frank thought for sure that Wally knew. It wasn't like Doug tried to hide it. Wally sat down in one of the chairs that was next to a small table and put his elbows on his knees and his head in his hands. Madeline looked at Frank and shrugged her shoulders. They waited for Wally to explode, thinking maybe his redneck pride had been violated in some way by riding in the car with a gay man. The blowup never came, Wally finally looked up.

"Well I guess his sexual desires are none of my business. He seems like a pretty nice guy to me." Frank couldn't believe Wally was taking the news so well.

"The Pink Pirate is right on Duval Street. You can't miss it," Madeline said, brushing her hair back as if she was getting ready to go.

"Wait a minute! Are you talking about the pink two-story building on the corner?" Wally said standing up.

"Yes, that's it," Madeline said slipping on her shoes.

"That's not a gay bar. A bunch of the dancing girls were out front last night when I walked by. They tried to get me to come inside and see some kind of dance revue."

Madeline bit her lip. "Those weren't girls." She said. Wally looked at Frank. Frank shook his head. Wally sat back down and put his face back in his hands. He was mumbling something.

"Wally you don't have to go with us if you don't want to," Frank said. "I'll understand, but you gave me an idea last night on how to find out what's going on here, and I need Doug's cooperation." Wally sat and thought for a second then stood up.

"I'd like to help out any way I can, but are you sure

those weren't women?" he said.

****

Anthony hung up the phone with room service. If he was stuck in Key West with a job to do at least he was going to eat well.

"Are you sure that was a hit man?" Paul said to his brother as he pulled the curtains a little tighter at the hotel room window. "He looked like some hick that works on cars or something to me." Anthony looked at Paul like he was an idiot.

"You dumb ass, he looks that way so you won't suspect him when he cuts your fucking throat open." Anthony ran his finger across his neck.

Paul pulled back the curtain just far enough to peek across the parking lot and down the street. Anthony shook his head and picked up the phone again. He dialed his uncle in Miami to report on their progress and maybe see about getting some back up, since the coke thieves now had a hit man out for them.

"We're gonna have to get some more men down here. There's too many of them and we've lost the boat." It was a good thing they were on the phone and not in Eduardo's office or he might have cut their throats himself.

"You screw ups, how did you lose the fucking boat?" he said between clinched teeth.

"It's not at the marina anymore," Anthony said.

"Maybe they're in the Bahamas setting up for the next shipment, you morons. Did ya ever think of that?" Eduardo was steaming.

"No, they're still here. Two of them tried to sneak attack us at the marina. If we hadn't seen them when we did they would have killed us in cold blood. We were lucky to get out of there alive."

For a brief second Eduardo thought how much easier life would have been if they had not been so lucky.

"I want you to get your ass to Bimini tonight, and keep an eye on the port there. Sooner or later, they have to show up. When they do I want you to hijack their fucking boat and bring it here to Miami. You got that?"

"You mean you want us to go outside, at night, without some more men down here?" Anthony tried to sound as tough as possible. It wasn't easy when you were afraid to go outside. Muffled curse words came from the Miami end of the line.

"Look asshole, just do what I told you to do!" The phone slammed down in Anthony's ear. Anthony looked at the ceiling and let out a sigh.

"We have to go to Bimini," Anthony said, as he set down the receiver.

"Now, tonight, in the dark?" Paul's eyes were as big as baseballs.

CHAPTER 23

Frank and Wally walking into The Pink Pirate together, was about as odd as a sixteen foot tall plywood alligator drinking beer from a mug. The lovely Madeline didn't seem to stick out at all. Frank looked around the dimly lit bar for Doug, but didn't see him.

"Maybe Doug isn't Doug when he's in here," Wally said, over Frank's right shoulder.

"What are you talking about?" Frank asked.

"Maybe he's Doris, or Delilah, or who knows what?" Wally answered.

"Oh shit, I didn't think of that. If he's in drag we'll never find him."

"If he's in drag, I don't want to find him," Wally said.

"The show starts in ten minutes gentlemen, just go right up the stairs there." A man with long dark hair and large breast wearing a long white evening gown split to the hip came up to them.

"Well, I guess I'm out of here," Wally said. "I'm not getting involved in any freaky sex show."

"No, no honey, it's nothing like that. It's a dance revue. Go on upstairs, you'll enjoy it," the dark haired person said, pointing to a flight of stairs off to the left of the bar.

"Well, well, well what have we here?" He was looking Madeline up and down.

"I'm a lady damn it, leave me alone." Madeline said.

"Hey we're all ladies in here sweetie. Some just pull it off better than others," the dark haired stranger said watching Madeline as she followed her partners up the stairs. The three of them found a table near the stage and ordered drinks from a Marilyn Monroe look-alike. When she brought the drinks Frank asked if she knew Doug and if she had seen him this evening. The waitress looked off as if looking at a distant memory.

"Doug, oh yes, I know Douggie very well." Coming back to reality she continued.

"He'll be back in a few minutes. He just had to run Monique back home to get her boobs. She forgot them." Frank handed her a five-dollar tip.

"Is he dressed, well, you know." Marilyn tilted her head side to side then finally caught Frank's drift.

"Oh, oh god no, he's one hundred percent man Doug is. Gay man, but no, he's no queen."

Wally was finding it hard to look anyone in the eye as he sat peeling the label off of his beer bottle.

"Sounds like our little Doug is quite the ladies man," he said as the lights went down and the emcee of the show came out on the stage.

"Welcome everyone. We're so glad you could come and spend the evening with us here at The Pink Pirate. Tonight's show will feature our girls dancing to the biggest show tunes of our times. Now, please help me welcome to the stage The Pink Pirate Dancers." He stepped aside and motioned with his arms as the curtain behind him raised and six or seven of the biggest women you ever saw danced arm in arm across the stage.

****

"We're gonna spend the whole night on the boat?" Paul was asking his brother as they drove down Duval Street heading to where their boat was docked.

"Yup and I'm getting tired of this shit. Tonight we take things in our own hands and put an end to it all." Anthony said as he brought the pickup to a stop at a red light. Paul looked out the window down a side street.

"Look! There's the car they were in at the marina," he said, pointing at a Toyota parked next to a pink two-story building.

"They must be at that bar. If we could sneak attack them tonight we could save ourselves a trip across the ocean," Anthony said. He wheeled the Chevrolet into a parking lot behind the bar. He noticed a back entrance as he got out of the truck. Perfect, he thought.

"We'll slip in the back so we don't make a scene," he said as Paul climbed out of the passenger side. Anthony loaded his pistol and stuck it in the back of his jeans, pulling his shirt down over it. The name of the bar was not visible from the rear entrance as the two gangsters made their way inside. They found a couple of barstools and ordered two glasses of beer.

"I don't see them, do you?" Anthony said. Paul had his attention on the tall dark haired lady in the white evening gown.

"Do you see any sign of them Paul.... Paul? Damn it Paul we're here on business not, jeez, would you look at the legs on her?" Anthony set down his beer.

****

The upstairs waitress brought Doug over to Frank's table when he returned from the boob mission.

"Frank, what are you guys doing here?" Doug said,

pulling up a chair.

"Shhhh, this guy's good," Wally said as a long-legged man in a black leotard danced to "New York, New York".

"Listen I have a plan and I need your help," Frank said almost in a whisper, not to disturb Wally's enjoyment of the fine art of a hundred and eighty pound man dancing in high heels.

"Boy, it must be some plan for you guys to come here looking for me," Doug said. The number on stage finished and Wally joined the conversation.

"Speaking of plans, I've got one before we get started. How 'bout we plan on you not kissing anyone while I'm here, Okay? Doug looked at Wally, then Frank. Frank spoke up, "we talked to the Marilyn Monroe character a while ago. She's kind of fond of you."

"Oh yeah, been there, done that," Doug waved it off like it was nothing.

"Oh jeez, I didn't need to hear that. Could we please get out of here?" Wally said, being about as good as a redneck in a bar full of drag queens could possibly be. The music started up again.

"Ladies and gentlemen, coming to the stage right now. Please welcome. Monique!" The emcee announced from the side of the stage.

"Wait, wait, wait," Doug said as the next dancer came through the small opening in the curtain. "This is Monique. She's the one that helped me with those assholes at your boat the other night. She's kind of like my steady. You know, like you and Madeline." He gave Frank a little jab in the ribs with his elbow.

"Nice boobs," Wally said jokingly. Doug didn't find the humor in the comment. 'Cabaret' was playing as a big person in a red sequined mini dress wiggled across the stage with a lime green feathered boa around her shoulders. Wally ordered a shot of tequila and another beer. Doug watched like he was looking at a goddess. Wally was looking for the waitress with his drinks and Frank was watching Madeline and thinking of her as his steady. Doug leaned over to Wally.

"Don't worry Wally, you don't have to participate, just tolerate." Doug sat back down laughing.

"Waitress I need that shot, please!" Wally hollered. Monique danced right up in front of Doug and put the boa around his neck.

"Oh you have got to be kidding, I can't watch. Waitress!" Wally was really starting to sweat.

****

Downstairs, during the Monique performance, Paul bought the dark-haired lady a drink, and was making small talk with her. Anthony had achieved eye contact with a redhead across the U-shaped bar. She smiled back and gave him a wink. Things were starting to look up for the guys in black. "With girls like this down here, what's the hurry to get back to Miami?" Anthony thought.

Monique finished her number and came off the stage to sit next to Doug. He introduced his friend to everyone and asked her if she would mind if they went someplace else for a drink, for Wally's sake. Monique said that would be fine with her. Madeline and Monique headed down the stairs as Doug, Wally and Frank followed. Anthony and Paul were too busy with their new found friends to pay any attention to the group coming down the stairs.

Soon they were on their way down the sidewalk stopping at the next bar they came to. The Rusty Anchor and was only a block away from The Pink Pirate. A man an woman were on a small stage, playing music that was popular in the sixties. The five of them found a table together, and ordered drinks ranging from a Budweiser for Wally, to a Shirley Temple for Monique.

"Doug here's the deal." Frank began. "Wally has got me to thinking that maybe I am running drugs, but I just don't know it. We think maybe they're sneaking them on the boat while I'm making the gold deal. I need someone to hide on the boat while I'm gone, and see if anything happens. You're the only person I know that is small enough to hide aboard the boat without being noticed."

Doug kept shaking his head, to let Frank know he understood the situation. Monique was looking at Doug like he was the bravest man alive, which was working to Frank's advantage.

"I'm going to make a run for Don tomorrow morning, and I'd like to have you on board. What do you think?" Frank waited to see what Doug would say. Monique spoke up first.

"Are those the guys that we threw in the bay Douggie?"

"Yeah, we think so," Doug answered.

"Well I think you should go, I lost a nail on account of them bastards." Doug nodded his head that he would defend his partner's honor.

"What time do we leave?" He said.

****

The drinks kept flowing at The Pink Pirate, to the point that if the men dressed as women, told the men dressed as thugs, that they were men, the men dressed as thugs either didn't remember, or they didn't care because the party kept going.

Doug made plans to meet Frank at nine in the morning at the marina. Then Monique and he went their own way. Wally didn't think it was too late to look for streakers, and since he had seen one the other night at the Island Breeze Bar. He thought that would be a good place to start. Frank finished his beer and asked Madeline to go for a walk with him. Of course she agreed.

He took her by the hand and they left the bar. Frank's heart was growing fonder of her every day, but he felt she needed to know the whole story about him, and let her make her own decision.

"Madeline," Frank spoke softy as the walked down Duvall Street. "I don't know how you feel about me, but I know how I'm feeling about you. It's tearing me apart. I haven't told you everything about me that you should know." Madeline didn't say anything. She walked quietly beside him, with her hand in his. Frank continued. "The reason why I'm not with Karen, my wife, is because she was killed in a car wreck a couple of weeks ago. I wasn't looking to get in a relationship with anyone for quite some time, but Don didn't know that when he set you and I up." Madeline pulled her hand away from his; he didn't try to take hold of it again. "Karen was one of a kind. She was everything I could have ever have dreamed of. We had been together for eighteen years. She was my whole life. Anything I ever did during those eighteen years I did for her. I felt the only way for me to be happy was for her to be happy, so I concentrated everything I had to please her." Madeline was starting to cry a little as they neared the Southernmost Point Monument.

"I never could have imagined she could be replaced and she can't," Frank went on. Madeline made a sniffling sound. "But you, you come along. The exact opposite of her, and I can't stop thinking about you. Karen is who I wanted to spend the rest of my life with, but that is now impossible. Time is the only way for me to get over her dying, and I may be a mess until that happens. If you could be patient with me, I promise to make you the happiest woman in Key West, if that's what you want." Madeline leaned back against the bullet shaped monument.

"Frank, I didn't know, I'm so sorry," she said softly.

"There's no way you could have. I should have told you up front," he said. Madeline stood still and brushed away a tear from her eye.

"I had hoped this wasn't going to be a one night event, but I don't know how long I'd be willing to wait in second place for you," she managed to say. Frank felt a tear of his own and didn't know if it was for Karen or Madeline.

"I understand, I'm sorry if I misled you." He placed the hotel and car key in her trembling hand and turned to head up South Street.

"Frank!" Madeline called out. He stopped and turned around. "Be careful tomorrow." Frank smiled at her, then turned and walked away. He caught a cab at the corner and had the driver take him back to his boat on Big Pine Key.

CHAPTER 24

Frank slept on the folded out sofa of the boat where Madeline had slept the night before. Sleep hadn't come easy, but Frank finally managed to drift off into a light sleep for a couple of hours.

A sudden rocking of the boat woke him. Someone had just stepped aboard the little yacht, as it sat moored behind Doug's friend's house. How the hell did they find me? Frank thought. They must have been watching him at Southernmost Point. Madeline, he had left Madeline alone, out on the street by herself. Damn, how stupid could he be?

Frank scrambled out of bed and located the chrome table leg that had to be removed when he changed the sofa into a bed. He heard footsteps coming across the deck of the rocking boat. He pulled the table leg back like a baseball bat but realized the ceiling in the small cabin would not allow him enough room to swing it. The handle to the hatch wiggled slightly. Frank had not locked it. Another stupid move, he thought. He held the table leg with both hands down by his side so he could ram it through the chest of whoever opened the hatch. Hoping the surprise attack would push them back far enough that he could make his escape.

The hatch slid open but only a few inches. Franks heart felt like it was going to pound its way out of his chest, banging against his ribs, like it had broke free from whatever attached it to whatever it was supposed to be attached too.

"Frank, Frank it's me Madeline." She slid the hatch open a little farther. Frank dropped the table leg, his eyes closed without him closing them, as he sat down on the bed.

"Frank, are you down there?" He reached over and turned on a small light.

"I need to talk to you," Madeline said, making her way down the steps. Frank fell back on the bed with his feet still on the floor.

"I'm so sorry about your wife. I know that has to be hard for you to get over something like that. I guess this relationship was kind of forced on you to begin with, I mean with Don setting us up without you knowing about it."

Frank looked up at her as she was pulling her large bra out from under her shirt. Frank's forehead wrinkled. What was she doing? She wasn't going to rape him, was she?

He spotted the table leg on the floor, in case he had to go for it. He imagined the embarrassing headlines. **Man fends off woman-attacker looking for sex.**

"I've decided I want to be with you, no matter what," she said slipping out of her shorts. Where's that table leg, this is going to be it, Frank thought. She stood there in her white panties and T-shirt for a moment before climbing into the little bed on top of him. Now, it was too late to defend himself.

"So I wanted to come by and just be close to you tonight." She reached up and turned off the light, then cuddled up next to him and went to sleep.

****

In a hotel room several miles away, the sun was beginning to peek through the closed blinds. Anthony and Paul were coming out of the drunken haze of last night. Anthony's pants were unfastened and Paul's shirt was on backwards. Beer cans and wine bottles were scattered around the almost destroyed room.
"Boy, did we have a couple of wild ones last night or what?" Paul said, just coming to with a pounding headache.
"The only thing I remember is, that bitch was fine," Anthony said, as he surveyed the room.
"Oh shit, we're supposed to be in the Bahamas!" Paul said, looking at his watch.
"Come on, let's get going," Anthony said, scrambling for his boots.

****

The early morning on the *Don't Worry* was sweet, as Frank opened his eyes to see Madeline's hair, with its fresh smell in his face. The sun was shining through the small cabin windows. He lay still, listening to her breath and felt the gentle rocking of the boat. He was happy that she hadn't killed him last night. Soon she stirred and kissed him.
"Good morning beautiful," Frank said.
"Morning," she said, still trying to wake up. "I'm glad I came here last night."
"I am too, even though you scared the hell out of me." Frank smiled.

****

On the way back to Key West in the little Toyota, they stopped and had breakfast and they went to the hotel. Frank walked Madeline back to their room and kissed her good bye at the door.

"Thank you for understanding," he said.

"You be careful today." Don't get yourself killed. You made me a promise and I'm going to hold you to it," Madeline said, not wanting to let go of his hand. Frank looked at her puzzled.

"You're supposed to make me the happiest woman in Key West, remember?" She pulled him closer.

"Of course I remember," he lied. "I'll be by to see you at the Captain's tonight, I'll promise you that too." They kissed again then Frank went down one floor to Wally's room. He knocked on the door and waited. No one answered so he knocked again. Soon a young lady opened the door wearing a man's shirt with just the bottom button fastened.

"Oh, I'm sorry, I must have the wrong room," Frank said.

"You must be Frank," she said and opened the door a little wider.

"Yes I am," Frank answered, and then he saw Wally behind her putting the last of his things into a duffel bag.

"You can keep that shirt babe. Maybe I'll see you again sometime," Wally said. The girl thanked him and began buttoning up the shirt as she walked out of the room with nothing else on, not even shoes.

"Wally you can't send her out of here dressed like that. She'll get arrested," Frank said stepping into the room as the girl started down the hallway.

"No she won't. That's one more thing she has on than when I met her," Wally said. It was almost like he wasn't the same person. He seemed younger more alive, almost cool. Frank decided he didn't want anymore details so he let it go at that.

"Let's go," Wally said, tossing the strap of the bag over his shoulder and walking past Frank, sliding a pair of sunglasses over his ears. Frank stepped out into the hallway.

"Hey, Joe Cool," Frank pointed, "the elevator is this way."

Frank dropped Wally at the bus station, and thanked him again for all he'd done.

"You know maybe I should stay and see if I can't give you and Doug a hand," Wally said as he pulled his bag out of the hatchback.

"No, you go on. You've helped enough. There's nothing else you could do. Doug's all I've got room for on the boat without looking to suspicious," Frank said. He left Wally waiting for his bus, promising to keep in touch. Frank went to Don Gold and Pawn to pick up the suitcase. Don wasn't open for business, but he was there cleaning up what was left of the mess and waiting for Frank. Don told Frank to be careful and asked about Madeline.

"She'll be fine," he said. "We have a room at the Beachcomber. I want her to stay there until things calm down."

"I'm glad you two are hitting it off so well," Don said. Frank explained to Don what was going on, and that this would probably be the last run of gold there would be.

"Well, if this is a drug smuggling cover up, I'd just soon it stop, I will miss the money thought," he said. "You say Doug is going to help you?"

"Yep, I'm going to pick him up now," Frank answered.

"Well you two be careful and good luck," Don said, as he handed the bag to Frank. Frank put the bag in the back seat of the Toyota and headed up Duval Street to Key Coast Marina.

Doug was sitting out front at a small picnic table drinking a Coke with another man. Both were dressed in walking shorts, T-shirts and rubber sandals with Velcro straps. Doug looked like a regular guy today. Sitting still and wearing something that didn't look like it would glow in the dark. You never would have guessed him to be homosexual. Frank wondered who the man was with him. He must be one of the other guys that lives aboard their boat at the marina, Frank figured. Frank walked over to the two men as they were getting up. Doug introduced Frank to his friend.

"I'm ready whenever you are," Doug said.

"Well, let's get going then," Frank said. Doug's friend was walking over to a red Honda when he called back.

"Hey Frank, by the way thank you for the drink last night." Frank waved it off.

"Don't mention it, Mark," he said. That couldn't be Monique, could it? Frank decided not to ask.

CHAPTER 25

On the way to Big Pine Key Frank, and Doug made sure they were not being followed. They talked about anything other than the voyage ahead. Once they arrived, Doug untied the *Don't Worry* and Frank went up on the bridge after putting the suitcase in the cabin. When they were out on the open water, after double-checking to make sure they weren't being tailed Frank decided to let Doug take command of the controls. Doug seemed to really get a kick out of steering the little yacht and paying attention to the global positioning screen. No other boats were in sight.

With Bimini on the horizon Frank took over and Doug made his way down into the cabin. He pulled the hatch closed and curled up on the floor near the steps. He wouldn't be seen if he sat on the sofa but he felt safer on the floor. Frank docked where he had the times before and unloaded the bike. When he went down into the cabin to get the suitcase he shook hands with Doug.

"Good luck," Doug said.

"You too, and don't do anything to get yourself hurt. Okay?" Frank asked.

"Don't worry, after all that's the name of your boat." Doug smiled, then retuned to his post on the floor. Frank couldn't help but wonder if he was doing the right thing, as he took off on the bike.

Doug could hear the voices of the fishermen preparing their boats, and tourist not far away along the shore. The sound of seagulls and the lapping of the water set Doug's mind at ease. Nothing was going to happen today. He began to settle back and felt that it was going to be a wasted trip for him, when he felt a sudden jerk of the boat. Not what he expected. It was not the feel of someone stepping off the dock onto the boat. It was the feeling of the boat getting bumped into by another boat. Then someone did step aboard. Doug stood up slowly and peeked out a small porthole looking out toward the stern of the boat across the deck. Outside on the deck the porthole was at about ankle level. Doug saw a set of work boots walking across the deck and then everything went dark. Something had been leaned up against the cabin, blocking the porthole. Doug tried to position himself where he could slide the hatch open slightly to get a better look, but decided it would be too risky. After all he was just a gay guy that worked at his dad's marina. He wasn't an FBI agent.

****

Anthony and Paul had not been sitting offshore very long when the boat they had been tracking for days pulled into Bimini. Anthony was watching through his binoculars when a red and yellow speed boat, much like the one he himself was on, pulled up and docked itself to the cabin cruiser. A guy jumped aboard the *Don't Worry* and removed a part of the deck's flooring. Then he went back to his boat and returned with a burlap sack.

"That's Ray, what the hell is he doing loading our cocaine onto their boat?" Anthony said. At this point Paul couldn't care less, he just wanted his head to stop hurting and get back to see his girlfriend at The Pink Pirate. Anthony pulled out his cell phone and quickly dialed his uncle in Miami.

"Guess who the fucking Bimini connection is?" Eduardo was in no mood for guessing games. Anthony answered the question himself. "It's fucking Ray."

Ray had been born and raised in Bimini. He was in his mid thirties and had been a lobster diver up until two years ago. Eduardo had flown over to the small island looking to hire a local who might be interested in making some fast money.

Twice a week a plane from Columbia would fly within three miles of Bimini's west coast at two o'clock in the morning. Ray was to take Eduardo's boat and go out and wait until the shipment dropped from the plane. He would then pick it up out of the ocean and run it to Miami before sunup.

Things had been working out great until Ray was approached by another man to make even more money without the risk of transporting the coke all the way to Miami. Ray started reporting to Eduardo that the shipments were no longer reaching him. Since he was the one to report the problem, Eduardo automatically suspected the pilot of the plane.

After closely watching the action of the pilot and repeatedly having him tailed on the drop missions all suspicions were dropped. Three of the largest coke dealers that Eduardo had been supplying in Florida let him know they were getting a better deal from someone else. So he knew the cocaine was getting to the drop off point in the Bahamas. According to Anthony it was being smuggled into Key West from there. The Atlantic in between the two islands had been the missing link. Now it turns out, one of his own men had been stabbing them in the back.

"Kill him," Eduardo said, and hung up the phone.

****

The object was removed from the view of the porthole. Doug felt the man leave the boat and heard an engine start up and pull away. Doug sat tight until someone else boarded the boat and slid open the hatch. It was Frank carrying the black case.

"Well, did you have any visitors?" Frank said, almost in a joking tone, he really hadn't expected anything to happen. Doug just nodded his head in an exaggerated motion. Frank stepped toward him.

"Let's just get the hell out of here okay, then I'll fill you in," Doug said.

"Okay Doug, just sit tight and I'll get us out of here." Frank could tell Doug was shaken, and got to the bridge as quickly as possible to head for the Keys. After a half an hour or so Doug came out of the cabin. Once the island slipped over the horizon they seemed to be alone. Doug climbed up to the bridge and told Frank what had happened. After a few more miles between them and Bimini, Frank shut down the engine. He followed Doug down to the deck. They felt around the edges of the floor until Doug located a small collapsible handle underneath the edge of the outdoor carpet near the stern. Frank looped his fingers though the handle and pulled on it but nothing happened.

"Turn it to your left," Doug said. Frank twisted the handle and felt it unlatch itself. He lifted the floor panel and set it aside. It revealed a compartment about four inches deep and covered half of the deck area. Frank reached inside and picked up one of the twenty to thirty brick-sized packages. Frank and Doug stood up looking at the package.

"How the hell did this get here?" Frank said.

"I just told you. A man came aboard in Bimini and…" Doug was cut off.

"No, not that, I know how that got there, but this," Frank said, referring to the hiding compartment. "How the hell did they know it was under here? Hell I didn't even know it was down here." Frank ran his hand along the bottom of the compartment where he had removed the package of cocaine. White residue was on his fingertips. He raised them to his nose. It was fiberglass dust.

"This compartment has been added to this boat lately," Frank said. "This is fiberglass dust, someone has been working on this area recently for fiberglass dust to still be here."

"The Magic Wizard! Remember," Doug began. "You said you'd seen their truck at the marina, and I've seen it there twice now. When I tried to call them the number was no good. They must have added this when you were gone someplace, and they unloaded the cocaine while you're at Don's pawn shop." Doug spotted a boat coming fast from the direction they had just traveled.

"Frank, look!" He pointed. Frank looked up and saw the boat.

"Here put this back." He handed the plastic-wrapped object to Doug and ran up the ladder to the bridge. The *Don't Worry* was up and running in no time, but there was no way they could outrun the pursuing boat. It was gaining on them quickly. Frank tried to radio for help but there was something wrong with the radio. Frank had neglected to test it. Doug put the package back with the rest of them and replaced the panel, and the carpet that covered it. He was now on the bridge with Frank.

Before long the speedboat had pulled along the side of the *Don't Worry*. Paul steered so close to them, Frank thought they were going to ram into him. Anthony held up his gun and ran his finger across his neck to give Frank the message to cut the engines, or he would start shooting. Frank idled down and cut the engines. As the cruiser settled into the water the speedboat did not stop as quickly. Paul looped it around and pulled up to their starboard side. Anthony threw Doug a rope and ordered him to tie it off. Doug grabbed the rope and did as he was told.

"Alright you mother fuckers, open up the cargo bay," Anthony said, as he stepped aboard the *Don't Worry*.

"We don't know what the fuck you're talking about," Doug said. Frank looked at Doug like he was out of his mind, but now he had to go along with his partner.

"Cargo bay, what do you think this is this is an ocean liner?" Frank said. Not knowing why Doug decided to lie, he'd rather they would take the cocaine and leave. Paul boarded the *Don't Worry*.

"Find the opening. It's at the back somewhere," Anthony said. Paul ripped up the carpet and found the latch. Soon they had the panel off and were tossing the packages onto their boat. Frank looked at Doug as they stood side by side with their hands in the air. Doug cut his eyes down to the cell phone on the waistband of his shorts to let Frank know he had contacted someone.

"You two are coming with us." Anthony said, pointing the gun at them. Just as they started to step across onto the other boat Doug stopped.

"Fuck you, I'm not going anywhere." Frank's heart stopped, climbed up into his throat and made him cough, then went back down to where it belonged and started beating again. Why in the world would a small, fragile man like Doug stand up to two thugs with guns, in the middle of the ocean, with nothing to gain? Then he saw where Doug got his courage. Two boats were speeding directly toward them. Frank figured Doug must have got through to the Coast Guard on his cell phone.

"Get the fuck on the boat before I feed the fish with your brains!" Anthony screamed, and pushed the gun barrel against Doug's temple. At that second the sound of the two approaching boats caught the attention of the gunman. The approaching boats were painted identically, pink with bright yellow lettering on the side. The lettering on the first boat spelled out The Pink, and the second one was named The Pirate.

Frank spotted Mark at the helm of the first one with Wally and two other men onboard. Four guys were on the other boat as well. They pulled up to the stern and the other to the bow. When Anthony saw Wally he tossed his gun onto the deck and put his hands down to his sides. Doug picked up the pistol and threw it into the ocean.

"The Coast Guard is on its way. They'll be here soon," Wally said. A man from the second pink boat, obviously a friend of Doug's, stepped across to the thug's boat and grabbed Anthony from behind. He twisted his arm into a position where Anthony was forced to his knees. Another of the Pink Pirate Army went aboard with a length of rope and started tying Anthony's hands behind his back as two other men did the same to Paul.

"Take it easy asshole. You're breaking my fucking arm." Anthony screamed. The man holding him down looked Anthony in the eyes.

"Well, well, what nasty language, last night you said I was beautiful, and reminded you of a fashion model. Ah, how soon they all forget." Another boat appeared off in the distance making its way toward the floating island made up of The Pink, The Pirate, The *Don't Worry*, and the gangster's boat. Anthony now appeared to be in shock from the new information gained about the wild time last night.

"Oh god, no! Say it isn't so, Anthony. Please say it's not true!" Paul pleaded, almost in tears.

A coast guard boat docked itself to the others. The captain was William Gardner. He took Frank and Doug aboard his vessel for questioning, and then allowed them to return to the *Don't Worry*. The cocaine was loaded aboard the coast guard's ship, and so were Anthony and Paul. One of the seamen from the coast guard boarded the thug's craft and piloted it back to Florida. Names and information from everyone was taken and Frank and Doug would have to report to coast guard headquarters in Miami tomorrow morning. Wally made his way onto the *Don't Worry* and everyone said good-bye to the men in the Pink Brigade as they headed back to Key West.

Frank sat down on the deck Indian style

"What the hell just happened?" he asked. Wally leaned against the gunwale of the boat and began.

"I was just about to get on the bus in Key West, when a strange wind blew through the bus station letting me know not to get on that bus, and to come and find you. Something bad was going to happen. I cashed in the ticket and caught a cab to Key Coast. When I got there you had already left, but I heard someone in a red Honda calling my name. I looked over at him but it was someone I'd never seen before. It turned out to be Mark who explained to me that last night he was Monique. Can you believe that was the same person that was wearing that red dress last night?" Wally said shaking his head.

"You should see him in blue," Doug chimed in. Wally shot him a glance.

"Oh, sorry, do go on," Doug said, trying not to laugh at his redneck friend.

"Anyway he told me that he had the same feeling, that you guys were in danger. That's why he had gone back to the marina to see if you two were still there. I jumped in his car and we went to Big Pine but when we got there the boat was already gone. So we went to The Pirate and called the coast guard. They said they had already received a call from someone aboard the *Don't Worry,* and were on their way." Doug cut in again.

"That would have been me, thank you, by the way it's the Pink Pirate." He patted his cell phone. Wally went on.

"Mark got permission to take the boats out and look for you guys. He's quite good with a boat, believe it or not."

"They use the boats mainly for parades, and sometimes to pick up big shot clients in Miami to bring them to Key West," Doug added.

Wally continued. "Some of the guys at the club overheard the conversation and thought maybe they should come along to see if they could help out. When we found you guys and saw the trouble you were in, we decided not to wait for the coast guard. Mark radioed them at that point with your exact location." Frank couldn't believe what he was hearing.

"Whatever it was that brought you and those queens out here, I sure am glad you came. I think they would have killed us if you hadn't got here." Frank said.

"Not all those guys dress up like women at night, do they?" Wally couldn't believe it.

"Yep, every one of them. As a matter of fact, Joe, the guy driving the other boat, he is the one that was dancing to "New York, New York" last night," Doug said, putting his hand on Wally's shoulder.

"No," Wally said, rubbing his chin. "No way, do you mean to tell me that I came all the way out here in the middle of the Atlantic and took on two drug dealers that had guns, and I was the only person on the two boats that don't go home and slip into a pair of pantyhose before he goes out?"

"That would be correct sir," Doug said; acting like his

smart-ass self again now that he was no longer about to be fish food. Wally decided it would be a good idea for him to sit down. Frank got up and shook Wally's hand and thanked him.

"You saved my life Wally, I'll never forget it," Frank said, and then he went up on the bridge and pointed the *Don't Worry* in the direction of Key West.

CHAPTER 26

As soon as the *Don't Worry* was back in its slip at Key Coast, Frank hailed a taxi to take him to Captain Crabbies. Business was slow as usual at the Captains on a weeknight. Usually the exact same people were at the same barstools and tables every night. When Madeline saw Frank come though the door she ran around the bar as fast as a woman her size on three-inch high heels could run. She threw her arms around Frank almost knocking him back out the door and onto the sidewalk.

"You're back! How did everything go? Are you alright?" she asked him between kisses.

"I was fine until I got here. I think you broke my back." Frank said laughing and rubbing his lower back. Madeline didn't crack a smile. Frank saw the concern on her pretty face.

"Well I guess you'd better bring me a drink, because this is going to take a while." Frank took a seat at the bar while Madeline got him a drink. She leaned against the bar as Frank told her everything. He told her about someone coming aboard the *Don't Worry* in Bimini, and about Wally and the pink pirates saving him and Doug from walking the plank. She didn't find it as humorous as Frank did, now that he was safe and sound back in Key West.

Madeline closed up the bar a little after one in the morning and they caught a cab together back to Key Coast. Frank was thinking that maybe he and Madeline could, after all, become more than just close friends. Frank paid the driver as the two of them stood in the marina parking lot. The marina was quiet and peaceful with little chance of gunfire this time. The only sounds were the lapping of the waves and the sound of a band far off at a more active bar than the Captain's had been. Frank put his arm around Madeline's big shoulders as they walked toward the *Don't Worry*. The little yacht had seen Frank though all of the madness. As large of woman as Madeline was, she felt fragile and delicate in Frank's arms. Her heels on the wooden dock made a classy sound. Frank stopped beside the boat and turned her toward him. She looked so gentle and sweet; he pulled her body close to his. Frank wanted to say he loved her, but knew it was not the right time, after his little speech at Southernmost Point last night. Her eyes changed, as if she knew what he was thinking as their lips touched. Frank felt a weakness in his knees this time. She was in his arms and he could think of no place else in the world he would rather be than standing on a dock in Key West, kissing Madeline.

"Oooooo, he's kissing a girl," Doug said from the bridge of the *Don't Worry*. "That's just gross." Frank broke away from the kiss but kept his arms around Madeline as he looked up at Doug.

"What the hell are you doing on my yacht?" Frank said, trying to sound angry but wasn't very convincing.

"We are par…tee…ann," Doug said holding up a drink and dancing like a girl. Frank noticed Wally and Mark up on the bridge also, like a bunch of guys sitting on a back porch someplace having a few drinks. Frank and Madeline boarded the boat as the three new friends made their way down to the deck. Wally handed Frank a Budweiser and Mark gave Madeline a watermelon wine cooler.

"Quiet a day wasn't it?" Wally said. Frank shook his head.

"Now that it's all behind me, maybe I can settle down into a normal lifestyle here in Key West."

Doug spoke. "Yeah, what could be more normal than sitting on a boat with a drag queen, a redneck, a gay guy, and a girlfriend that could kick all our asses if she wanted to?"

Madeline threw the screw-off cap from her wine cooler at him. It harmlessly hit him in the chest and fell to the deck.

"What?" Doug said, shrugging his shoulders. "Stop me when I'm lying."

"If you're looking for normal, you're in the wrong place," Mark said. Frank took a long swallow from his beer and then looked Madeline straight in her eyes, as she leaned against the edge of the boat.

"I'm not sure what I'm looking for, but I know I'm in the right place," Frank said, as a strange wind blew across the bow of his boat.

Jeffery Lamb is a native of Florida and currently lives in Lake County with his wife Sherri. He has a true passion for the Sunshine State and its mix of interesting people. He has recently purchased a 32 foot catamaran sailboat that is kept in Daytona Beach. Writing is quickly becoming a favorite activity for him and more tropical adventures are sure to follow.